Hideout

Cal Mason has a price on his head and a posse on his tail, but it looks like his luck has changed when he makes it to Shorty Prentice's hideout. The trouble is the old man's cabin is already occupied and when Cal turns down an offer to join the Hinds gang he finds he has enemies on both sides of the law.

It would have been a good time to cut and run, but it's too late for he's fallen head over heels in love with Shorty's daughter. With another outlaw determined to steal his girl, Cal has one heck of a fight on his hands.

And then there are the lawmen baying for his blood!

Hideout

Eugene Clifton

A Black Horse Western

ROBERT HALE · LONDON

ISBN 978-0-7090-8308-5

Robert Hale Limited
Clerkenwell House
Clerkenwell Green
London EC1R 0HT

Typeset by
Derek Doyle & Associates, Shaw Heath
Printed and bound in Great Britain by
Antony Rowe Limited, Wiltshire

CHAPTER ONE

The horse had been dead a couple of days, and the scent of rotting flesh hung heavy in the air. Scavengers had already moved in to feed on the carcass; in the parched heat it wouldn't be long before there was nothing left but a few bleached bones.

Cal Mason turned to look at the other body, his lean face grim beneath the two-week growth of beard. He'd only known Shorty Prentice for three months, but he'd come to see him as a friend. They'd shared a camp-fire, yarned over a drink. And together they'd outrun the posse that had been on Cal's tail.

For a while after that it had looked like they were in the clear. They'd jogged peacefully westward, until Lady Luck ran out on them; the law picked up their scent again, and a few days later Shorty's mare took sick. It had been Cal's idea to split up. Shorty would try to make it to the hills, while Cal led the posse on a crazy chase across a hundred miles of prairie.

Unlike the horse, the cause of the man's death was easy to see: a small black-rimmed hole made an extra eye in his forehead, a little to the left of centre. There were powder burns around the wound; it had been inflicted at close range.

'You dumb fool,' Cal murmured, bending to pick up the .38 that had dropped from Shorty's hand, after he'd fired that last fatal shot. 'You could've waited for me.' Cal glanced back the way he'd come, knowing he was the fool, not Shorty. He couldn't blame the old man for not wanting to die at the end of a rope. A cloud of dust hung over the group of riders who were still dogging him, pressing him hard. His horse couldn't carry two, not with a posse on its heels.

Turning to face the high ground to the south-west, Cal sought out the three notches outlined against the sky. At a guess they were still more than a hard day's ride away. The middle notch marked the trail he had to reach, the one Shorty had described to him before they parted.

Close to, the crack in the rock would widen out to become a narrow canyon, and when a man rode through he would find the walls closing in, the gulch ending in a tumble of stone too rough and steep for a horse. But if he turned to the right, passing a jutting outcrop ten times his own height, he'd find a track that zigzagged up the bluff and onto a ridge. Reach that and he'd be safe, unless somebody on that posse wanted him badly enough to risk following him into country where every rock provided cover for an ambush.

A familiar face came to mind, that of a man who might be ready to take that risk. Cal shook the thought away. Maybe Shorty's friends would be keeping watch from the lookout; they'd have the drop on anyone who rode uninvited through the gap in the hills. Trouble was, that might include Cal Mason.

Cal's horse stood ground-tethered a little way off, tearing ravenously at the parched grass, its rough black coat turned grey-brown by a layer of dust and dried sweat. It was thinned down, hard muscled and fit, but it couldn't go much further without food and rest. Glancing at the approaching dust cloud Cal decided now was as good a time as any to let the horse eat; he'd make time to do the decent thing by Shorty Prentice.

Sliding Shorty's .38 into the front of his belt, Cal leant down again, this time closing the staring eyes. A small package stuck out of the dead man's top pocket. Cal pulled it free. A piece of string held a dollar bill around the outside of an envelope. On this, having crossed out his own name and an address in Denver, Shorty had written three words in large clumsy letters: ELIZA PRENTICE. KENTVILLE.

Cal tucked the envelope, still with the dollar bill attached, into his vest pocket. Kentville wasn't far away, but his chances of going there, or any place where he could use Shorty's last dollar bill to mail the letter, were pretty slim. Working fast, with half an eye on the progress of that menacing column of dust, he wrapped Shorty's body in the bedroll that lay beside it. There wasn't time for a proper burial, but he gathered rocks to pile over the man's remains.

The posse would probably dig up the body again, just to check that it wasn't him lying dead in the dirt; they'd be disappointed, but he hoped they'd have the decency to rebury the old man. Cal's lips twisted in a sour smile. The distraction might win him a few more minutes.

'Don't reckon the coyotes'll get you,' Cal said, standing up after placing a last stone on the grave. Across the prairie he could make out tiny black specks at the base of the dust cloud; the posse were getting too close for comfort, but he'd started this, he'd finish it right.

'Well, Shorty, I'm supposed to say a few words, I reckon, though there's only me and him to hear.' He nodded in the direction of his horse. The skinny black lifted its head, its ears pricking in his direction before it returned its attention to eating, tearing the dry fronds as if its life depended on it.

'Never got the hang of this kind of thing,' Cal went on, taking off his hat. 'I guess I just want to say goodbye. Not much point me trying to put in a good word with the Almighty, seeing as I'm likely headed for the other place, but wherever you end up, I sure hope there's a friend waiting for you.'

Cal sat easy in the saddle, the black covering the ground in the steady lope it had kept up ever since he left Shorty's resting place. As the day drew near its end and the shadows lengthened, the posse were no longer dark dots but horses and riders. They were gaining on him, but there was a good chance they wouldn't narrow the gap much more before the sun dropped below the horizon.

Once it was dark he would need luck, and that had been in short supply the last few days. He couldn't afford to stop and wait out the night. Unless he reached that middle notch the next day, he'd be joining Shorty real soon.

Soon the ground beneath the black's hoofs could only be guessed at. Cal eased back from a jog to a walk. For a long time the horse plodded on in the darkness, stumbling now and then. There was no light to be seen; only a few dim stars shone overhead. If the posse had stopped they hadn't lit a fire. Most likely they were still moving, just as he was.

Cal stared up at the sky and cursed; cloud had covered the last of the stars, even the bulk of the mountains on the horizon had disappeared. He could go on, but he'd probably ride in circles. At the faint twitch on the rein the horse stopped, head drooping in weariness. Sitting quite still, Cal listened. He heard nothing.

Lifting down, Cal slackened the cinch and took off his hat. Groping for a canteen he poured water into the hat and let the horse drink, then he reached into the saddlebag, bringing out a handful of grain and tossing it on the ground. The black twitched its ears and lowered its muzzle. When its meagre meal had gone it lifted its head and butted against Cal's shoulder.

'I'm getting soft,' Cal muttered, but he felt around for a second handful. Cal couldn't recall when he'd last tasted decent food. He chewed on a strip of jerky, trying to imagine he was chomping on a piece of prime steak. A few mouthfuls of water from the canteen completed his supper. Three nights back he'd risked lighting a fire, keeping it going just long enough to brew coffee, but to do that tonight would be madness.

With no stars showing he could only guess how much of the night had gone. It was probably no more than four hours to dawn. His body yearned for sleep, but he daren't lie down. The posse would take turns to sleep and keep watch, but if he let his eyes close he couldn't guarantee he'd awaken with the sun, not when he was so close to exhaustion. If he overslept then the next sunrise could be his last.

Beside him he could feel rather than see the black. Its meal finished, it stood relaxed with one hind foot resting and its head drooping. Cal ached from head to toe, and he reached out to the bedroll, almost ready to take the risk. The horse shifted its weight to the other hoof, moving the blanket away from his hand. 'Yeah,' Cal said, 'I know. Hell, if you're so smart how come you couldn't wake me up when there's light enough to go on?'

He felt in his top pocket, though he'd run out of tobacco days before. His fingers encountered the envelope he'd taken from Shorty. He couldn't see the words in the dark but he remembered what they were. Eliza. That would be Shorty's daughter. To keep himself awake Cal began to go over the story Shorty had told him.

The place in the hills Cal was heading for had once been Shorty's home. All this big land had been truly wild then, and Kentville just a two-bit trading post, a place without law. The nearest town of any size was Silverlode, five days' ride away.

Shorty looked wistful when he spoke of the ranch he'd carved out of the wilderness. Civilized folks thought he was crazy, but in those days few people knew about the remote valley. Lawless men felt safe in Kentville: they didn't need to take refuge in the canyons, and nobody else discovered the high pasture hidden in the hills. Shorty and his wife lived there in peace, just the two of them, until their son was born. They named him Mike, after his father. Cal hadn't even known Shorty's given name until the old man told him that.

They were good times, Shorty said, as he stared into a past Cal couldn't see. A couple of years after Mike, Eliza had come along, and made things just about perfect.

ORDER FORM

HOW TO ORDER

- Select products and complete order form
- Take to your nearest store
- Hand in your form, confirm details and pay

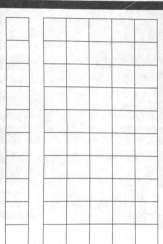

CODE						QTY

Shorty was driving a small herd of cattle to Silverlode each year, and getting a good price for them.

Then one winter the snow came early. The world turned hard and cold. They were ready for it, well provisioned and snug, until little Mike took sick with a fever. Despite all their efforts to care for him, the boy got worse. In desperation Shorty finally wrapped the child up in a cocoon of blankets and lifted him onto the front of his saddle. With a spare horse and a good supply of food he'd ridden out into a blizzard, heading for Silverlode. It took him over a week but incredibly, he'd made it, arriving with the boy still clinging stubbornly to life. But his wild ride had been for nothing. The doctor couldn't save the child, and little Mike died the next day, just four years old.

'And that was the end of it.' Shorty had taken a long pull at the bottle of whiskey before handing it back to Cal. 'My wife plumb refused to stay up in the hills. Wouldn't risk the same thing happening to Eliza. Can't say I blamed her, but it came hard, walking out on all I'd done. We moved to Silverlode, and I set up a little gunsmithing business. I'd learnt the trade in the army, and it made us a living. Later we shifted to Kentville, seeing it was starting to grow into a decent kind of town, but I didn't feel right, stuck there with all those folks. My heart wasn't in it. Finally I closed down the store and rode out on a cattle drive. When it was finished I sent the money back home rather than go myself.'

They'd sat in silence a long time, and Cal had thought Shorty had nothing more to say, but then the older man sighed. 'Funny ain't it, how easy a man can drift off the road. I'd been an honest man all my life, but when work got scarce I took up with Dobey Hinds, and before I knew it there was a price on my head. I never did get back to Kentville. Heard a couple of years back that my wife had died. Eliza was taken in by some neighbours. Good, God-fearing folks they were, family by the name of Sears. At least I knew she'd be well looked after. Can't help thinking about her, though, wondering how she looks now she's growing up some. Last time I saw her she was seven years old, long-legged little squirt, with freckles on her face and hair as bright as sunshine. Guess she must be nearly as tall as me by now.'

Cal came awake with a jerk, almost falling as his cramped leg muscles twitched. He'd been back at that campsite by the river with Shorty. Or had he been in Kentville, handing a letter to a little girl with freckles dusting her nose, and bright braids hanging over her shoulders?

He stared into the darkness, hoping for some sign that the dawn was coming. Maybe one day he'd make it to Kentville. The men who'd tracked him so relentlessly couldn't stay on his heels forever; Shorty had sworn nobody could reach the valley without being seen by the lookout. He was sure the posse wouldn't be fool enough to attempt it, not when rumour said there could be half-a-dozen desperate men hiding out up there.

According to Shorty the tally right now was only three, but those three would be enough to deter any sensible lawman. Cal had never met Dobey Hinds, or the Rodway brothers, who rode with him. Bart Rodway had a bad reputation, and they said his younger brother Moke wasn't far off crazy. When Shorty told him the Hinds gang were holed up in the hills, Cal had a mind to go someplace else, but by then the pair of them were out on the prairie with the posse pushing them hard; it was no time to be picky.

Cal shivered. After the heat of the day the night was chill. The black was awake, head down to pick at the odd blades of grass beneath its feet. Lifting his canteen off the saddlebow Cal took a drink and tried to convince himself that he could see a little further into the darkness. Maybe the dawn wasn't far away.

The cold of the night wasn't even a memory. All was heat. A shimmering haze obscured the view of the hills; had those notches come any closer? For hours a merciless sun had beaten down on the baked earth, and the black's hoofs sounded loud in the silence. Even the rush of air on Cal's face as the horse loped across the endless prairie was furnace hot. The black was wet with sweat, white foam flecked its chest and flanks, and its breath came in desperate hard gasps as it laboured on. Cal's pulse was racing. He didn't need to look back; only one solitary rider had stayed with him, the others falling back rather than risk killing their horses.

Facing front again and staring into the heat-haze, trying to figure out how far he still had to go to reach the hills, Cal leant lower on the black's steaming neck. A shiver ran down his back, despite the heat. Such dogged persistence made him wonder if that relentless enemy was somebody he knew. He had come so far, fought so hard to stay out of the posse's clutches, but now for the first time Cal wondered if he was going to make it.

CHAPTER TWO

The race was for the highest stakes; life or death. Every ounce of Cal's body was focused on riding light and easy, resisting the temptation to look over his shoulder for fear of throwing the black off its stride; the horse was close to finished by the long hard chase.

At last, thinking the pounding hoofbeats behind him had slackened, he took the risk and glanced back. A sudden beat of hope pulsed through him; he was opening up a lead. The chestnut his pursuer rode was heavy built, more like a plough horse than a cow pony. It had stamina, that was why it had pushed him so hard, but in this last desperate race he doubted it could match the black.

A few moments later Cal took another look. The distance between the two of them was lengthening, slowly but surely. It was an uneven contest; the following rider was built on similar lines to his mount, while the months spent on the run had thinned Cal down to nothing but skin and gristle; the black had a lot less weight to carry, and over a distance that made a difference.

'Come on, I always treated you fair,' he urged, crooning the words like a love song into the slicked back ears. 'Another half-mile. You can do it. Just get me to that valley

14

and I swear you can rest for a month.' As if it understood his words, the black found a last reserve of energy, and there was something triumphant in the rising rhythm of its hoofs as it pounded towards the dark line of high ground that reared up ahead of them. They were so close now that Cal could make out the hard shadows thrown down across the splits and crevices in the rock as the sun sank westward.

The rest of the posse were out of the race, left far behind. Most of them had pulled up, coming on at a jog, knowing that for them the contest was over. Only the solitary rider was a threat. Cal was grimly determined that he wouldn't be caught, no matter what it took he wasn't going to be strung up on the nearest tree, or dragged back to Bannack County for a mockery of a trial.

Once the black carried him into that dark shadow under the hills the horse could take a breather; only a fool would ride after him. He could take his time covering that last mile, climbing to the ridge then dropping down to Shorty's cabin. He'd be watched by unseen eyes, the outlaws tracking him, maybe not trusting this stranger riding into their midst, but with the posse so close on his heels he reckoned they'd let him through, and maybe even help him keep the lawmen at bay.

Where the cliff didn't dissolve into sharp shadows, the rocks glowed with yellow light from the sun, reflecting the day's merciless heat at him. At last the ground was rising beneath the black's hoofs, and there before him was the jagged fissure, no more than the breadth of two wagons from one side to the other, just the way Shorty had told him. Inside, it narrowed even more, with cliffs rising high to either side, and it turned a little so he was riding into shadow.

Cold air hit horse and rider like a shower of rain after the hammer blows of the sun, and Cal gasped. The cool was welcome, but the black faltered, and for a second Cal thought it was going to fall. Maybe it was the shock of the sudden change of temperature, or going so swiftly from such brightness into shade; most horses hesitated before they entered the midday darkness of a barn.

Urging the horse on, breathing a relieved sigh when it recovered and jogged on a few strides, Cal glanced round. His pursuer wasn't far behind, already plugging up the slight rise in the ground, only yards from the entrance to the canyon. Cal leapt off the black, swearing as the animal balked, hauling it behind him to take shelter behind the jutting outcrop Shorty had described, where the shadows lay even deeper.

They were in cover. The black heaved in painful breaths, blood trickling from its nostrils as its head drooped. Laying a grateful hand on its neck for the briefest moment as he dragged his rifle from its boot, Cal left the horse and climbed up the rock and into a narrow fissure where a split in the stone made a natural defence. Wordlessly he gave thanks to Shorty; his friend's advice was about to save his neck. Glancing at the opposite cliff, he half expected to see the watcher he knew must be up there somewhere, but the rocky landscape offered a thousand hiding places, and he saw nothing.

Cal heard the man who was following him before he came into sight, the sound of the approaching horse picking up an echo from the hills. It jogged, its pace ragged and faltering, and its breath roaring. Hitting the shadow it seemed to shudder, but unlike the black it didn't recover, and its knees buckled. The poor beast was foundering, ridden beyond endurance.

The rider stepped out of the saddle and away when his mount fell, a rifle appearing in his hand as if by magic, his head swivelling. He was intent only on hunting down his quarry, the horse forgotten. Cal cocked the rifle and lowered the barrel slowly until he had the man full in his sights.

As the man lifted his head to scan the rocks he could see the features beneath the tilted brim of the hat. It was the face of a stranger. A young man, clean shaven, maybe not old enough to be needing a razor. He made a big target, moving slow, turning a little to continue his search of the hillside, as if unaware of his danger. Cal gradually tightened his finger on the trigger, drawing in his breath, waiting for his racing heartbeat to steady. At such short range he couldn't miss. A full five seconds passed, then the sound of the shot echoed around the hills.

As the bullet lifted a spurt of dust from the ground at the young man's feet he jumped, bringing the rifle swiftly to his shoulder. The youngster stared into the shadows, his gaze roving across the place where Cal was hidden and moving on. As if provoked by the sound, the exhausted horse lifted its head. Cal had thought it was dead, but it rose unsteadily to its feet and took a couple of steps back towards the sunlight.

'Your horse has the right idea,' Cal shouted. 'That shot was just a warning.'

'You can't run for ever.' This kid, the last persistent remnant of the posse, was either very brave or very stupid. He stood out in the open, full in Cal's sights. Cal bit down on his lip, knowing he could end things in the blink of an eye, yet reluctant to kill this crazy stranger.

'The next one won't miss,' Cal called back. 'Best get out of here.'

The youngster shook his head. 'Why don't you come down and save us all a lot of trouble?'

Despite himself Cal gave a short bark of laughter. 'You got some nerve, kid, I give you that. Fact is, you're the one with the trouble. Giving myself up don't seem to recommend itself to me, though I guess there must be something in it for you.'

'Two thousand dollars,' the youngster said.

Cal almost rose from his hiding place in amazement. 'You're joshing me.'

'Got the poster right here in my pocket.' He seemed to have located Cal now, and the rifle was pointing his way. 'Someone's going to claim that reward, might as well be me.'

'I never figured anyone would put that sort of price on my head,' Cal said. In some twisted way the thought amused him. In all his life he'd never had that much money, even when the ranch was doing well. 'If you're aiming to be a bounty hunter there's a few things you need to learn. Look behind you. Those coyotes know better than to follow a man once he's got the high ground.'

The youngster was acting so crazy Cal had thought for a moment he was there to provide some kind of diversion, but the rest of the posse were keeping their distance. Three of them had halted well out of rifle range, staring into the shadowy ground where the canyon narrowed. They could maybe make out the madman who stood facing him, though Cal was pretty sure they wouldn't be able to spot the rocky fissure where he was holed up.

Behind them the stragglers were still riding in.

'Let me tell you something else,' Cal went on. 'Something you need to learn if you plan to live a while longer. It's hard to collect bounty money when you're dead. Right now I could put a bullet in you any time, I'd say that puts you at a disadvantage.'

'Your first shot missed.'

'I told you, that was a warning. Could be I'm getting soft.' When Cal spoke again his voice had an edge to it. 'But I don't like being pushed, kid. I maybe won't kill you, long as you don't keep on riling me, but you'll find it hard, riding with a bullet in your leg or your arm, even if that horse of yours is fit to get you out of here.'

There was a silence, going on so long that some of the tension began to ease out of Cal's muscles; his whole body was aching with the need for rest. He wanted sleep. The longing for it grew with each passing second, becoming so powerful he was close to losing his temper. He would end this. Squinting along the barrel, Cal drew in a breath and squeezed the trigger.

The young man leapt a couple of steps backwards, shocked into motion as the slug flung the hat off his head. He stumbled as he landed, putting a hand to his scalp and seeming surprised to find no blood there.

'No more warnings. I'm running short on patience,' Cal said. 'Get out of here, and take that plough horse you nearly rode to death back to the farm where it belongs. Go on, git, before I give you what you're asking for.'

The youth bit his lip as if trying to think of a reply, then he turned slowly, picked up his hat and stalked away. His horse stood waiting for him, splay legged. He gathered up the trailing rein and pulled the animal into motion, heading back to join the cluster of men, all now dismounted and watching from a safe distance.

Cal watched for some time, hearing the low murmur of voices but unable to make out what was said. Pretty soon the riders began unsaddling. It looked as if they were planning to make camp; the shadows were lengthening and it would be dark in a couple of hours. Feeding the horse a generous helping of grain and the last of his water, Cal watched while the posse tended their own mounts and lit a fire, then he moved on.

The track was just the way Shorty described it, winding up to the narrow ridge. Cal led the black, hauling it on the end of the rein. They made it to the high ground, and although he was terribly weary there was a kind of contentment settling on him. By the time darkness fell he'd be safe in Shorty's cabin. The posse could go to the devil. He'd hide in the hills, either alone or with the Hinds gang, for as long as it took for the rest of the world to forget about him, and that $2000. Cal shook his head, disbelieving what he'd heard. The kid must have got it wrong; he doubted if even Dobey Hinds was reckoned to be worth that much.

Although the sun was low in the sky, up here in the open it was still unbearably hot. 'Last stretch,' Cal said, straightening his back in an attempt to ease the ache from his spine. The black heaved a human-sounding sigh.

It was the exhausted horse that saved him. Some finely toned sense warned it, maybe a stray scent or the click of a hoof on a stone. The animal jerked forward in alarm, its shoulder brushing Cal's arm when he was off balance and knocking him halfway to the ground.

As Cal fell, a spray of hot wetness hit his face. He scrambled back to his feet with the horse almost pulling the rein from his grasp; it wanted to run from whatever had caused the sudden stab of pain in its neck. There wasn't time to think, only to act. Cal's hand grabbed the high saddlebow and he swung himself up, half hearing the crack of a second shot. With all his attention focused on guiding the black across the treacherous terrain, loose rock sliding beneath its hoofs and threatening to bring them both down at every stride, it was almost a minute before Cal dared to take a look back over his shoulder. It was the youngster, a rifle in his hands, riding like a madman, lashing at the big-boned plough horse that came plunging after them, its exhaustion apparently forgotten.

Cal was suddenly filled with a cold anger, the fear of a moment ago distilled into something far more deadly. He had held that man's life in his hands, and twice he'd pulled back from firing the fatal shot. He'd been a fool; pretty soon he might pay the price.

Freedom was so close; as the black surged on he could see down into the hanging valley where Shorty's cabin stood squat and square, a little way beyond the top of that impossible tumble of rocks above the narrow canyon he'd ridden into a while before. The steep slopes of rock went on, so the building almost filled the gap between them, the weathered grey timber shining with a gold sheen in the last of the light. Somctime soon he must find the track that led down to the cabin; ahead of him the ridge climbed, becoming increasingly steep and rocky, he doubted if a mountain goat could get up there, let alone a man on a horse.

The wound in the black's neck was still spraying blood,

21

but the bullet had only nicked the flesh, and the panicked gallop had slowed to a weary lope. Another shot, snapped off in haste from the back of his pursuer's horse, cracked past them, making Cal duck. The butt of his rifle was under his hand, but he let it lie for the moment and crouched lower over the blood-streaked mane.

A deep gully, formed countless centuries before when the mountains were still in motion, opened up only feet away from the black's hoofs, crossing the ridge and barring his way.

'Jeez!' Cal had forgotten this last defence, though Shorty had told him about it. The horse, weary as it was, veered in response to the urgent shift of his rider's weight. Even as he began to turn to the right, where a narrow track hugged the top of the precipice, Cal knew it was too late. The crevasse was a little narrower here though, and clapping spurred heels to the black's sweat-streaked flanks, Cal urged it to one last effort. The poor jaded beast had been close to finished an hour ago, but it wasn't ready to give in. Hoofs scrabbling for purchase, the black made a desperate leap for the other side of the chasm.

CHAPTER THREE

There was a terrifying glimpse of the rock-scattered cleft below, plunging far down through the mountain to his left. On the right the gully was shallower, but equally deadly. Cal flung his weight forward as the black soared over the gully, and time slowed, with the horse poised on the brink of disaster. He was ready to throw himself from the saddle in a last desperate attempt to save his neck, yet instinct made him hang on, made him urge the horse with a shout of encouragement and a frantic thump of his spurs against its ribs.

The black's hoofs scrabbled for purchase on the treacherous slope, loose stone tumbling, rattling, the sound growing fainter as the rocks bounced and rolled hundreds of feet down the mountain. Somehow getting a hind leg to the ground, the animal bunched its haunches; with every muscle and tendon straining, it gave a great heave and lunged up to level ground and safety. Or the illusion of safety. A bullet sang, ricocheting off the rock away to their right, making the black leap to a gallop again. The young madman on the plough horse was still behind them, and closing the gap.

Cal had always considered himself an even-tempered man, but there were limits. The horse's great lurch out of the gully had almost thrown him. Heaving himself back, he pulled the Henry rifle from its boot, his eyes seeking out a rock, no matter how small, to give him the cover he needed. Another shot zipped by and he ducked, cursing.

In all this landscape of dust and stone there was nothing that would hide a man, not up here on the ridge, nor on the track which must soon lead down towards the cabin. Cal realized with sudden bitterness that the crevasse he had risked death to cross would have given him cover, but it was too late for regret; if there was nowhere to hide then he would make his stand in the open.

Giving himself no time to change his mind, Cal checked the black and leapt out of the saddle before it came to a halt, his hands working the Henry's action as his feet touched the ground, his trigger finger snugged round the hot metal. He would take his chance, and hope the youngster didn't have the sense to take cover in the crevasse that split the ridge in two; if he did Cal would make an easy target.

The rifle was at his shoulder, but before he could take aim the big ungainly horse reached the brink of the crevasse. Seeing the sudden drop into the chasm yawning at its feet, the chestnut threw its head up, forelegs bracing, trying to slew aside, but it had been moving too fast, and it wasn't built for quick turns.

Horse and rider fell together, the beast letting out a great scream that was abruptly cut off. If the man made any sound Cal didn't hear it. There was a crash and a rattle of stones, and a heartbeat later a rushing sound as the last trickle of dust fell. Then silence.

Cal straightened, letting the rifle swing down in his right hand. Glancing back he saw that the black had come to a halt and was watching him, one wary eye rolling. Cal made a harsh sound with his tongue and the horse came, its sides heaving, the blood still dripping from the wound in its neck. Cal ran a gentle hand down the animal's sweat-streaked shoulder and replaced the rifle. Only a dozen yards from where they stood the trail began its descent, winding downhill. He could see the roof of the cabin, half-hidden by shadow.

The sun was close to setting, its light slanting along the ridge. Lifting to the saddle Cal pushed the black into motion. Could be the Hinds gang weren't there right now, or maybe they figured his fight was no business of theirs. He didn't like the idea of riding in uninvited, and it would be dark soon.

Cal had gone no more than a dozen paces before he stopped. With a curse at his own soft-headedness he turned and went back to the cleft which had so spectacularly rid him of that last stubborn opponent. He stepped out of the saddle.

Like him the kid had angled to the right when he saw the gully open up at his feet. The crevasse narrowed swiftly there, and the body of the big horse lay jammed across it only a couple of yards down. Beneath it, all Cal could see of the youngster was one leg in faded grey pants, and a dusty boot. Carefully he climbed into the gully, until he could reach to touch the leg behind the knee. A pulse beat steadily under his fingers.

'Jeez!' Cal straightened. The horse was three-quarters of a ton of dead weight he couldn't hope to shift. He eased his way to the other side of the animal, uneasily aware of the drop at his back. Bending down, he found the young-ster staring up at him.

The kid's eyes, narrowed with pain, met his. 'Damn you!'

'I'm not the one who rode his horse to death,' Cal said,

'you made a proper job of it this time, broke his neck.'

Some fleeting emotion swept across the youngster's face, but was quickly wiped away. 'It would have been worth it if I'd killed you,' he said.

Cal leant in to get a closer look, lifting the horse's mane aside. The only visible damage was to the kid's other leg, bent back beneath the animals' shoulder. 'Reckon you can feel that leg.'

There was a curt nod. 'Bone's busted I guess. It hurts, if that pleases you any.'

'Sure does,' Cal said. He grinned at the venomous look this won him. 'Means your back ain't broke. Any chance you can haul yourself out of there?'

The youngster struggled to get his elbows to the ground and pushed; he didn't shift an inch, though the effort drew new lines of pain on his face. 'Dammit, Jacob,' Cal heard him mutter, 'looks like you got your own back.'

Cal climbed up to level ground again. He didn't have a rope, but he took the leathers from the black's saddle, then he went back down into the crevasse and removed the dead horse's bridle, tying it to the one stirrup he could reach.

'If I can shift the weight it's up to you,' Cal said shortly, a few minutes later, heaving back to test the strength of the tangle of harness.

How they did it Cal could never quite figure, but minutes later the young man lay white-faced on one precipitous side of the cleft with both legs clear of the horse's body, while he and the black stood on the rocks above, breathing hard. All three of them were drenched in sweat.

Cal stood figuring his next move. If he got the black

back across the cleft then it would have to make the perilous journey yet again, maybe in the dark. It wasn't worth the risk or the effort. He left the horse ground-reined.

With the sun almost resting on the horizon, Cal lifted the injured youngster over his shoulder and set off back along the ridge and down the winding trail. Not far from the place where he'd shot the kid's hat off, he stopped and lowered his burden to the ground. He'd taken the precaution of removing his prisoner's six-gun from its holster, and now he emptied the chambers, leaving both gun and bullets a few feet away.

'Take you a while to reach that, but I reckon if you fire a shot and shout loud enough they'll maybe come up and find you. If not you'll have to crawl,' Cal said, nodding towards the posse's camp. 'They had the sense to know when they were licked. You must have been real desperate for that two thousand bucks.'

'I don't give a damn about the money,' the youngster said. 'Mort Bailey was my uncle.'

'Your uncle?' Cal looked at him appraisingly, trying to see something familiar in the broad features and brown eyes. He shook his head. 'I know Sheriff Macomber. Don't reckon he ever had a son.'

'My name's not Macomber. I'm Seth Bailey, same as my pa. Mort was my pa's brother. I was on my way to start work at the Bar Zee when you shot him.'

'So you were going to work at Mort Bailey's ranch?' Cal hunkered down at the youngster's side. 'Reckon you and me got some talking to do. You may not exactly be kin to Glenn Macomber, except by his sister's marriage, but you can take him a message just the same.'

*

Cal led the black towards the cabin, feeling like a new-born calf walking into a wolf's den. He had wanted to do this in daylight, when the outlaws could take a good look at him; creeping in at night wasn't a great idea. A quarter moon gave just enough light for him to be seen. Rocks beside the trail were blacker shapes against the darkness of the coming night. Just out of easy rifle range from the cabin he came to a line of thorn bushes, uprooted and pegged in place with stakes. Cal lifted his hands and held them out, showing he held no weapon.

'I'm a friend of Shorty Prentice,' he called, coming to a halt at the barrier. Looking across the thorns he could see a solitary dark window staring back at him. There were two others, both shuttered, and from what he could see in the shadows he thought the door was closed. There was no sound. 'Anyone home? My name's Mason. Shorty told me I'd find friends here.'

A metallic sound cut the silence. Somewhere to his right a rifle bolt was drawn back. The voice, harsh and low, came from the same direction.

'Drop your holster. And step away from the horse.'

Cal couldn't see the man who'd spoken, nor the other one who was coming up from directly behind him, though the hairs on the back of his neck told him somebody was there. Slowly he unbuckled his holster and let it fall, and he moved a couple of paces away from the black, until they were separated by the length of the rein.

'Let the horse go.'

Reluctantly Cal did as he was told. 'Real good of you boys to welcome me this way,' he said. 'Figure Shorty would be pleased to know you made me so much at home.'

'Shorty knows the score.' The man who'd spoken was coming closer. 'He knows better than to send strangers here.'

'I'm a friend of his. Rode a long way.' Cal lifted his empty hands. 'You got my guns. How about we go inside and talk? There's fresh coffee beans in my saddle-bag.'

A man, nothing but a dim shape in the near dark, came from behind him and grabbed something in the thorn hedge, pulling a section aside, then moved round him to disappear again. 'Go on through. Right up to the door.' It was the same voice as before.

Cal obeyed, ears stretched. He heard the shuffle of footsteps. The black was led in behind him and the barrier closed. At the cabin door the procession came to a halt.

'Open it. Walk right in.' Again he did as he was told, taking three steps into total darkness before he stopped. Behind him there was the scrape of a match, and a flare of light that settled into a steady glow as a lamp was lit. 'Get the shutter, Bart. You can turn around now, mister.'

Facing him, holding a carbine with its deadly black eye pointing at his head, was a man with grizzled grey hair and a starkly white moustache. Wearing a fancy waistcoat and sporting a gold watch-chain stretched across a generous belly, he looked like the kind of man you'd meet walking his grandchildren to church on a Sunday morning. Cal recognized him from a poster he'd seen years before; Hinds was a notorious outlaw, wanted in four states.

'You'll be Dobey Hinds.' Cal took a step backwards to put a little more distance between them, then held out his hand. 'I'm Cal Mason. Shorty told me about you.'

Hinds hesitated no more than a moment before he lowered the carbine and shook hands. 'Can't place you. Don't reckon you've ridden with anyone I know.'

'Only Shorty. Met up with him three months ago. I was on the run with a posse on my tail, and they didn't want to let go. If it wasn't for Shorty I'd be nothing but crow bait by now. We lost them, but a couple of weeks back the law picked up our tracks again.'

'We heard a couple of shots. They follow you here?'

'One of them did. He only got as far as the ridge, don't reckon the rest of them are stupid enough to try and ride in here.'

'So where's Shorty?'

'Dead. We had to split up a week back, when his horse took sick. Did my best to lose the posse and give him time to get here, but it was a bad move. All I did was win a few hours, and I found Shorty with a bullet in his head. That was a couple of days ago.'

'You saying the posse got him?' Hinds's eyes narrowed.

'No. I guess he got tired of running, or maybe he could feel the noose tightening around his neck. He shot himself.'

'You got any proof of that?' The other man's voice was hard as he moved in, his fists bunched. This had to be Bart Rodway, Cal decided; what he'd heard hadn't been far wrong, this wasn't somebody he'd willingly turn his back on. Rodway was a stocky dark-haired man with cold blue eyes and a week's growth of beard. He jutted his stubbly chin at Cal, looking for trouble.

'Kind of hard to prove a thing like that,' Cal said, keeping his tone even. 'You'll have to take my word for it. He left a letter for his kid.'

Hinds sent Rodway a warning look and nodded slowly. 'Can't say I'm surprised; you get to know when a man's had enough. I reckoned Shorty was close to the end of his tether last time I saw him. You planning on staying a while?'

'Sure was hoping you'd ask me,' Cal replied.

'There's food and bedding for your horse in the barn behind the house. You take your turn keeping watch, and if you want to eat you help make the meals.'

'I'm a pretty good hand with a frying pan,' Cal replied, 'but I feel like I've hardly slept in a month. Hope you won't mind if I catch up on some shuteye.'

'Sure. Go tend your horse then we'll eat,' Hinds said. He nodded at Bart. 'Go with him and see he's got what he needs. And bring in that rifle he was toting.'

Half an hour later Cal was back in the cabin, his hands wrapped round a mug of coffee, his bedroll tossed down in a corner of the room. 'That tastes good. Didn't get to light a fire the last few days.' He glanced around the cabin. 'Snug place. I'm real grateful to you for taking me in. A man gets tired of watching his own back.'

Hinds nodded. 'We'll be here for a month or so, then we've got a little venture planned, down in Silverlode. Be a hand adrift without Shorty. Maybe you'll want to join us.'

Cal took a sip of coffee. 'Maybe,' he said.

The cabin door crashed open, and a man strode in. Moke Rodway was dark and stocky like Bart, but unlike his brother, Moke had very pale eyes. They were almost silver, hot and constantly in motion, like molten metal. The newcomer launched himself across the room. His mouth twisting with anger, he swung his clubbed fists at Cal's head.

CHAPTER FOUR

Cal crashed to the floor. If he hadn't thrust out an arm to soak up some of the sheer ferocity with which Moke delivered the blow, it would have killed him. With his head ringing and his balance gone, he had just enough sense left to keep moving, and he took the kick Rodway aimed at his kidneys on his thigh, grunting with the force of it, rolling fast under the table to get himself out of range.

Slamming into the legs of the stool Bart Rodway was sitting on, Cal snaked his body under the table, half afraid the man might try to finish what his brother had started; he was relieved when Bart made no move, though it sounded like he was laughing. Shaking his head in an attempt to clear away the fog, Cal struggled to his knees, keeping the heavy wooden boards between him and Moke.

'What the hell?' Cal demanded furiously. It was suddenly very important that he get on his feet, though if the outlaws had decided he was an enemy it would be an empty gesture; Hinds' carbine leant against his chair, and both the Rodway brothers wore six-guns slung low on the hip. Cal's Smith & Wesson hadn't been returned to him, and his rifle was out of reach, propped against the wall; he figured Bart had probably removed the slugs anyway, when he fetched it from the barn.

Which left Cal out of options. Driven by desperation he heaved himself upright, staggering a little. He bunched his right fist; there was no feeling in the left, the whole arm numb from Moke Rodway's first blow. 'Is he crazy?' he shot this at Hinds, still seated at the end of the table in the cabin's only chair.

The man shrugged, evidently no wiser than Cal as to the reason for the attack. 'Well, Moke? That's a strange way to say howdy when a man comes calling. You got something on your mind?'

'I sure have,' Moke Rodway snarled, not taking his eyes off Cal. 'He's a lawman.'

'He's what?' Hinds sat up straight, his eyes suddenly ugly and his features hard. He no longer looked like anybody's kindly grandpa.

Cal laughed, a grim sound, full of the bitterness the last three months had sown in his soul. 'You are crazy,' he affirmed. 'And I've got something here that'll prove it.' He reached to his shirt pocket. Tucked behind Shorty Prentice's letter was a handbill. He'd taken it from young Bailey before he left him, and now he shook out the folds and offered it to Hinds, keeping a wary eye on both Rodway brothers.

'What's it say?' Bart demanded, scooting his stool across the floor so he could look over Hinds' shoulder. 'Hey, that's him!'

'Wanted dead or alive,' Hinds read, 'Charles Aloysius Mason, otherwise known as Cal, wanted for the murder of Mortimer Bailey. $2000 reward, offered by Sheriff Glenn Macomber of Bannack County.'

Bart Rodway whistled. 'Two thousand bucks!'

'Yeah!' His brother laughed, a high-pitched yipping sound like a coyote. 'Hell, that's gotta be a fake. An' how about that name. Aloysius! Ain't nobody called that.' In a split second he was serious again, his mouth twisting, his strange luminous eyes alight. 'I'm tellin' you, he's the law. Now I see him close I know it for sure. I seen him before. He was with the posse that hunted down Wally Yeldon two years back. Take a good look at him, Bart, you was there.'

Bart grabbed Cal by the arm and jerked him around so he could stare into his face, drawing his .45 with the other hand. 'You have that bill made special so you could trick us? Figured you'd be collecting a bounty, huh? Or maybe you're gonna tell us Moke here's a liar?'

'I'm calling nobody a liar,' Cal said. He was still dizzy from Moke's sudden attack, and it was an effort to stay upright, but it wasn't the time to show weakness, and he met the outlaw's glare, steely eyed. 'Sure, I rode as a deputy a time or two. It's no secret. They were paying three dollars a day, seeing as how nobody wanted to go after Yeldon.' He pulled back to free himself from Bart's grasp. 'Jeez, that's no big deal, I needed the money.'

'He could be telling the truth,' Hinds said, watching Cal narrowly though he was talking to Moke Rodway. 'The way he tells it, he knew Shorty right enough. I had him figured for real.' He gave a slow smile, his expression suddenly benevolent again. 'Might surprise you boys to know I rode with a posse myself once, long ago. As Mason says, it can pay well.'

'He wasn't makin' no money when he saved the neck of that deputy up on the ridge,' Moke said, stepping in closer to spit the words in Cal's face. 'If'n he was on the run he'd have left him to rot.'

'What happened up there?' Hinds asked. 'Mason said one of the posse came after him and nearly killed his horse, but if that's not the way it happened. . . .'

Bart Rodway raised his Colt .45 so the end of the barrel was resting under Cal's jaw, an unpleasant grin fixed on his lips. 'Go ahead, little brother, Mason ain't gonna say a word.'

'It looked like he'd outrun that posse, only one man followed him onto the ridge, an' fired a couple of shots when he was nearly at the gully. Could be one of 'em creased that bag of bones he was ridin'. Anyways, he made it across the gully somehow, but the deputy's horse fell. Sounded like he took half the mountain down with him.' He nodded, his strange hot eyes boring into Cal's. 'Wasn't much chance the *hombre* would still be alive. When Mason went back I figured he was plannin' to put a bullet in the sonovabitch, just to make sure of 'im, but he went climbin' down an' brung him back out. Took him back to the trail so the posse could come fetch him.'

'Moke's right,' Bart said, 'that stinks. Besides, if he was ridin' with Shorty he shoulda known how to get over the gully.'

Cal's eyes were hard as he faced Moke. The effects of that knock on the head were still with him.

'You got nothing to say?' Hinds asked.

'Shorty told me about the gully,' Cal said, 'but I forgot. I was busy trying to save my neck. Then when the kid fell I decided I might as well make use of him. Told him to take a message for me,' he went on, as Bart Rodway jammed the gun barrel harder against his neck, 'to Glenn Macomber.'

35

'He was the one posted the reward,' Bart said, 'What in hell would you wanna say to a man who put a price on your head?'

'Macomber's sheriff of Bannack County, but he wasn't with the posse. I wanted him to know what would happen to anyone else who was fool enough to come after me,' Cal said.

'If Mason was working with the law why'd that man follow him onto the ridge and risk breaking his neck in the gully?' Hinds said reasonably. 'He'd have given up like the rest of them. And that bullet could easily have hit Mason instead of his horse.'

'Real strange this Macomber didn't come after you hisself,' Moke said, still suspicious. 'Seein' he was the one posted the reward.'

'I asked the kid about that,' Cal said. 'Seems there was some trouble at Beale River and Macomber had to go chasing off down south. He deputized the kid to keep tabs on me, along with a handful of townsmen. Said if they didn't track me down he'd fetch me himself when he had the time.'

'Still figure it stinks, you helpin' a lawman,' Moke growled.

Cal shrugged. 'He was just a kid who thought riding with a posse was easy money. Sure, I could have killed him, but why waste the lead? He's young enough to learn sense.' He summoned a grin. 'Look at me. Like you said, two years back I was riding with Macomber, sworn in as a deputy to help track down Wally Yeldon, risking my neck for three dollars a day. Now I've made it big, I'm hiding out with Dobey Hinds and the Rodway brothers.'

'So maybe the kid will end up our side of the law, huh?'

Moke seemed pleased with the idea, and for the first time since he'd flung the door open he was looking at Cal with something other than suspicion. 'I like that. Makes sense.'

'Then maybe I can get another cup of coffee to make up for the one you washed the floor with,' Cal said. He yawned, easing back against the wall to keep himself upright. 'Then I'd sure like to catch up on some sleep.'

'Well?' Hinds looked at Bart, then Moke. 'What do you say?'

Bart shrugged. 'You're the boss.'

Moke nodded. 'Sure.' He smiled without a shred of friendliness. 'It ain't like he can go noplace.'

Cal slept almost two days through, then Dobey Hinds told him it was time he took his turn on watch. He returned Cal's rifle, though it came with a single slug. 'All you have to do is fire a shot,' he said. 'We hear it, we'll come running. But that posse took off yesterday, don't reckon they'll be bothering us.'

The sun burnt down out of a clear sky, furnace hot. Cal spent three long and tedious days perched in the lookout, where a slab of rock overhung a hollow in the hillside, giving a precious patch of shade. He sat cradling the Henry, staring at the shimmer of heat over the prairie; this was where Moke had been the day the posse had chased him into the canyon, watching through an ancient telescope.

The fourth morning Cal finally saw something. A small herd of buffalo, maybe fifteen of them, were headed across the prairie, not far from the notch that led into the canyon. He fired off his single shot. Bart Rodway came riding at a gallop up the hidden trail to join him, and returned just as fast, whooping and hollering, calling his brother to join the chase. From his high vantage point Cal watched them, not impressed when they ended up with only one carcass, and that an old and scrawny beast. The resulting steak didn't taste much better than the usual salt bacon and jerky.

Time dragged on, days growing into weeks. It would have been a relief to go hunting, but Hinds always sent Moke or Bart when he had a fancy for fresh meat. Cal began working around the cabin, fixing a leak in the roof, mending the pump handle. Things had hardly been touched since Shorty Prentice left, but there were tools in plenty, and it beat playing yet another game of poker for nickels and dimes, with Moke accusing the others of cheating every time he lost a hand. Moke had a short fuse, and several times Hinds had to step in to calm him down when he tried to force Cal into a fist fight.

When he could find nothing else to do in the cabin Cal moved out to the barn, and set about replacing the broken door, one eye usually on the mountains that ringed the valley. He watched the eagles that flew high overhead, seeing them swoop down as they hunted small animals in the long grass. Sometimes he'd see deer coming to drink from the river that still ran with clear cool water despite the summer heat. He was beginning to understand why Shorty had been so attached to this place. If Hinds had trusted him he might have ridden out to explore the wide grassland that stretched into the valley behind the cabin, but he was only allowed to ride to the lookout.

'What you doin' that for?' Moke demanded suspiciously, finding Cal smoothing down a plank of wood.

'Because it beats hanging around scratching my backside,' Cal replied easily. 'It's something to do. Helps the time to pass.'

Moke grunted. 'Guess I get what you mean,' he said. 'You know what I miss, bein' cooped up here? Whiskey an' women.' Those strange bright eyes stared unseeingly at the hills. 'Whiskey an' women,' he repeated wistfully. 'A man can get too much of 'em, more than's good for him maybe, but it sure comes hard doin' without. Wish Dobey would let me go to Silverlode. Plenty of both down there.'

'I recall he spoke about going sometime soon,' Cal said. 'Maybe you won't have to wait much longer.'

'What he's figurin' to do won't get us no women, not straight off anyways,' Moke replied with a grin. 'But I sure mean to grab me a few bottles while we're there.'

It was only a couple of days later that Dobey Hinds came looking for Cal in the barn. He leant against the open door, watching Cal hammer in a nail.

'Something I can do for you?' Cal asked.

Hinds nodded. 'Guess you're about ready for some action. Fact is, I can't keep the boys cooped up here any longer, Moke's about ready to explode. We're going to hit Solomon's Bank in Silverlode. Three men can do it well enough, though I figured Shorty might be riding with us. If you want to take his place you'll get ten per cent. If it goes well you can ride with us regular, quarter shares. What do you say?'

'Guess it's kind of an honour to be asked to ride with the Hinds gang,' Cal said. 'But there's something I have to do in Kentville first. This letter's been burning a hole in my pocket all this time, reckon I owe it to Shorty to see it gets delivered.'

Hinds nodded. 'Fine. We'll all ride out tomorrow. You

head for Kentville, and soon as you're done come on down to Silverlode. Meet us in the Ace of Spades in six days' time. I'll be picking up some extra horses on the way, so I don't figure we'll be there much before you.'

'Remounts?' Cal asked. 'You got a long journey in mind?'

'Only back here. But it means we don't have to worry about killing our horses if we ride out of town with the law on our heels.'

'Good idea. Where are you leaving them?'

'You'll know that when we get there,' Hinds replied. 'It's a safe place. There's a man I can trust who'll take care of them.'

'You trust him but you don't trust me,' Cal remarked mildly.

'You've given me no reason to trust you yet,' Hinds said. 'Maybe this little trip to Silverlode will change that.'

CHAPTER FIVE

The black was fresh after weeks of going no further than the lookout; it kicked back at Moke's pinto as they rode down the narrow trail. 'Hey, quit that,' Moke yelled. 'How come he's ridin' with us anyways?' he asked, turning to Hinds.

'Could be he's giving us a hand in Silverlode,' Hinds said, 'seeing we don't have Shorty. We'll see.'

'You mean you told him what we're doin'?' Bart spat into the dust.

'No. I mean what I say. Could be he'll give us a hand. But first he's going to Kentville, while we go fetch some horses.'

Cal glanced back at the notch in the hills as they rode away, almost sorry to be leaving, despite the weeks of boredom and Moke's unwelcome company. He didn't expect to see the hidden valley again. Shorty Prentice had made it a good place, a home for his family until tragedy drove them away, and working there had brought Cal a kind of contentment. On the other hand he didn't care if he never spent another day with the Rodway brothers. He hadn't said as much to Hinds, but he wasn't about to help them rob a bank, in Silverlode or anyplace else.

They parted when the sun was a great red ball balancing on the horizon, Cal spurring the black to a gallop, thinking he'd reach Kentville before dark, then he changed his mind, making camp a couple of miles outside of town. Could be the posse had passed this way, since young Bailey was in need of a doctor; if by some chance the law in Kentville was looking for him he didn't want to ride in when it was too dark to see his way out again. His horse would be fresher in the morning too, ready to run.

Hinds was taking a long route to Silverlode, and Cal thought he knew why, from snatches of talk he'd overheard between Bart and Moke. They were going to cut the telegraph wires between the two towns, supposedly to hamper any pursuit, but Cal guessed Hinds wasn't yet ready to trust him. They'd be watching the trail. If a lawman headed out of Kentville to warn the marshal in Silverlode then the raid would be abandoned, and he'd have Hinds and the Rodway brothers looking for him with murder on their minds.

Cal grinned to himself as he lay staring up at the stars. He had no intention of talking to the law in Kentville, but he wouldn't be joining Dobey Hinds' gang either. Once he'd delivered the letter to Shorty's little girl he was heading north.

The message he'd sent with young Seth Bailey wasn't likely to change anything, and he didn't want to be running from Glenn Macomber for the rest of his life. He'd heard there was a welcome for a man in Canada, and not too many questions asked. The time he'd spent working on Shorty's cabin had been restful, reminding him that he didn't object to doing an honest day's work, given the chance.

After the weeks in hiding Cal didn't look much like the picture on the handbill he still carried in his top pocket; he'd been clean shaven when he lived in Bannack County. He rode into town early and found the barber's shop, where he had the man trim his hair, but not too short. He kept his beard, just having it tidied up some, then he paid for a hot bath. Next he went to the store and bought a shirt, bright with blue and red check; it would distract folks from looking too closely at his face.

Smelling strongly of soap, Cal was ready to carry out Shorty Prentice's last wish. Reluctantly he passed a saloon, where a man, yawning and stretching, was just unlocking the door; it didn't seem the right place to go asking after a respectable family.

Along the street a man in black was also unlocking his door. Cal looked around. He counted at least a dozen places where he could buy a beer, but it looked like Kentville had only one church. 'Excuse me, Father,' he said, touching the brim of his hat. 'Would you happen to know where I can find a man by the name of Sears?'

The Sears house stood well back from its neighbours in a neat yard. Cal was glad to find Shorty had been right; it looked like these were prosperous people. Little Eliza would be well cared for. At the front was a porch, swept clean and completely bare. With the front door closed, and the windows hung with heavy brocaded curtains the house looked uninviting, not the sort of place where a stranger might expect a warm welcome.

A little daunted, Cal took a narrow path that led round to the back. Here there was a smaller door, unpainted and beginning to warp. Lifting a hand to knock, Cal suddenly froze. From inside came the sounds of an argument, raised voices shouting words he couldn't quite make out. Something smashed as it was thrown against the door.

It was still early. Cal looked around; there was nobody in sight and he couldn't be seen from the street. He moved closer, putting his ear to the warped planks. A man was cursing, not very fluently but with great venom. Maybe this wasn't such a good home for Shorty Prentice's little girl after all.

'Don't you touch me!' The next words came from a woman, her voice taut with anger. 'You think I haven't noticed how you look at me when nobody's watching? All this time I've put up with it, the way I put up with her nagging and bullying.'

'Amelia has always been fair.' The man sounded as if he was trying to keep his voice down. His accent spoke of money and an Eastern education. 'I don't understand how you can say these things. You should be grateful. We gave you a home. . . .'

'You call this a home? You gave me nothing but the clothes I stand up in, and look at me. And then there's the days I went hungry because I maybe didn't run quick enough when she called me. . . .'

'It was sometimes necessary to discipline you—'

'And how you enjoyed it!' she broke in on him. 'I used to see you watching while she beat my hands raw. And next day she'd drag me out of bed at dawn to wash clothes, making sure I used plenty of soda. Did you ever try that? It's like scrubbing your fingers with poison ivy.'

'We took you in when you had nowhere else to go. . . .'

'Yes, that's true. It was this or one of the saloons. I let you turn me into a slave because the only other thing I could be was a tramp. And now you've pulled me down so low you think I'll give in to you. Well, you're wrong. I won't be turned into a whore, not now, not ever.' There was desperation mixed with the fury now, yet the voice was attractive, and Cal found himself wondering what the woman looked like. 'Come any closer and I'll scream so loud the whole town will hear. I'll tell them the sort of man you really are—'

'You think you'd be believed? A gutter brat with no father, and whose mother died of some filthy disease—'

'How dare you! My mother was a good woman and you know it. She went on working long after she should have taken to her bed. She did that for me, because she loved me.' For the first time the woman's voice faltered and it sounded as if she might be crying. 'You're nothing but an animal! Keep away!'

There was a loud metallic clang, as if somebody had struck a large gong, then the door was thrown open and a young woman bolted straight into Cal's arms, only to recoil from him and stumble back over the threshold, her face blanching white.

Cal followed her inside and closed the door behind him. A man dressed in a dark business suit lay on the scullery floor. He was fat, with a fleshy face and drooping jowls, and he appeared to be out cold. Beside him lay a large flat frying pan.

The woman backed up against the far wall, one hand to her mouth as she stared at Cal. He stared back. She was much younger than he'd expected, hardly more than a girl. Her hair was tied up in a black bandanna, which framed her oval face to make it look even more shockingly white. She wore a baggy dress in shades of brown, too big, and worn into tatters at the hem. Despite that he thought she was the most beautiful thing he'd ever seen. Although she was a mite thin, her figure curved in all the right places; her skin was flawless, and her large eyes were a stunning shade of blue.

At that moment she darted into motion, as if to dash past him to the door. Letting her go running into the street seemed like a bad idea, and he blocked her way. 'Take it easy,' he said.

She began to sway on her feet, a strange distant look in her eyes. Cal caught her before she fell and lowered her into a rickety old chair that stood in a corner. 'Take a good deep breath,' he advised, 'you'll be fine.'

'I've killed him,' she gasped, her hands lifting, the fingers covering her mouth as she stared with horrified fascination at the man on the floor.

'I doubt it. You stay right there a minute.' Cal bent down, and checked for the man's pulse, then felt the breath blowing warm from his nose and mouth. 'He'll be coming round in a while I reckon. His name Sears?'

She nodded.

'I was afraid of that.' Cal looked around, then peered through the internal door, which led into a room so full of furniture it was hard to imagine the fat man negotiating his way around it. He could see no sign that a child lived in this house. Maybe Shorty had got it wrong. From the way these people treated their help it didn't seem like the right place for the orphaned daughter of an outlaw.

Sears stirred and gave a low moan. At once the young woman jumped to her feet, reaching to pick up the frying pan.

'No,' Cal said, taking it gently from her hand. 'Not that

I don't sympathize, but you might do some permanent damage next time, and you don't want to end up in gaol.'

She shuddered and sank back into her chair. 'I don't know what to do,' she whispered.

'Where's his wife?'

The young woman looked up at him. 'She's visiting with her sister in Silverlode.' Her stark white cheeks were suddenly suffused with colour. 'You heard what we were saying. . . .'

'Guess I did.' Cal gave an apologetic shrug. 'I'm sorry. I'd say you'd better get out of this house, and soon. There must be some other place you can find work.'

'Dressed like this?' She asked bitterly. 'I stayed because I didn't want the only other job a girl can do in this town.' Her chin tilted up, thought there was a quiver in her voice as she went on. 'There's a man at the Silver Dollar who'd take me in, he spoke to me on the street a few weeks ago—'

'No!' The word came involuntarily, before Cal could stop it.

'What else can I do?' She asked. A solitary tear ran down her cheek and she brushed it furiously away.

Cal chewed on his lip. This was none of his business. If it hadn't been for Shorty's letter he never would have come to this house. The girl would have had to find her own way out of this mess. He sighed, remembering that moment on the ridge when he'd decided to pull young Seth Bailey out from under his dead horse; he never had the sense to stay out of other folks' troubles. And it looked like he still had to find Eliza Prentice.

'How long have you worked here?' Cal asked.

'Five years and two months,' she said. 'I know exactly, you see, because it was the day after my mother died.'

Cal felt something between disappointment and relief. He'd begun to wonder if he might have miscalculated, and that this could be Shorty's daughter, more grown up than he expected. But the outlaw had told him his wife had died just a couple of years ago. Still, he'd do what he could for the girl, before he dealt with his own errand.

'They never paid you a cent in all that time?'

'No.' She gestured at the sack-like thing she wore. 'And they didn't waste any money on my clothes either, I have to make do with her cast-offs.'

Cal hunkered down beside the man on the floor, who had rolled over onto his back and had his eyes half open. Before they flickered shut again Cal was sure he saw awareness in them. He grinned, seeing the way out. 'Then they owe you five years and two months in wages. I'd say that must be quite a sum, wouldn't you, Mr Sears? Guess you always meant to do the right thing by this woman, but you never got around to it.' He gave the generous stomach a none-too-gentle poke. 'What do you say?'

Searsilet out a gasp of pain. 'Don't! I didn't ... We didn't—'

'Mean to be so mean,' Cal finished for him, the grin widening. 'Sure. How about five dollars a week? I don't rightly know what's fair. A cowpoke gets more than that, all found, but you can't be too generous, or folks will say I was twisting your arm. And we don't want that, do we? What do you think?'

'Five dollars. Very fair,' Sears said hurriedly, giving Cal a sidelong look. 'Yes, indeed.'

'And an extra month's pay, because you didn't give her notice to leave,' Cal added, beginning to enjoy himself. 'Then a hundred on top of that, as a kind of apology, because you tried to take advantage of her.' He shook his head and tutted. 'That ain't polite.'

The young woman was staring at Cal as if she didn't quite believe what she was hearing, her hands at her mouth, the fingers pressed to her lips. 'But. . . .'

'You earned every cent,' Cal said, rising to his feet. 'You got a piece of paper so we can work it out? Then me and Mr Sears will walk over to the store, where he'll buy you a dress that's fit for you to wear to go to the bank. He can take you along to fetch your money, you won't need me for that. Of course he'll write a chitty tallying up exactly what he's paid you, and why. And he'll give you a reference to say how well you worked all these years, so you'll be able to get another job. Won't you, Mr Sears?'

The fat man hesitated.

'Of course, if he doesn't want to make things all nice and legal then we'll have to go to the sheriff's office, where he'll be charged with rape. Pretty careless, trying a thing like that with a witness outside the door. Maybe he can persuade the law that he's not guilty. After all, he only meant to rape you, maybe it makes a difference that he didn't succeed, seeing how you fought him off. Still, I don't think his wife will be too pleased. It's bad for a man's reputation when he gets dragged into court for something like that.'

'There's no need!' Sweat was starting on the man's face. 'I'll pay her. And I'll give her a reference. Eliza has always been—'

'Eliza?' Cal stared down at him, then at the young woman. 'You can't be Eliza Prentice!'

CHAPTER SIX

The girl looked at Cal, a little frown appearing between her brows. 'Yes, I'm Eliza Prentice. But what's that to you? How do you know my name?'

'Jeez!' Cal felt as if he'd been punched in the stomach. 'I came here looking for you! Only I thought . . . I was expecting a kid, twelve years old maybe. When Shorty . . . when your father told me about you, about his little girl, well, heck, I didn't think you'd be so grown up.'

Cal twirled his hat in his hands, trying to find a way to explain. 'From what he said, I didn't think your mother had been gone so long,' he ended lamely.

'My father sent you?' The lines on her forehead had deepened and there was a new strength in the way she held her head. This was the young woman he'd heard fighting for her honour, the one who'd flattened Sears with a frying pan. 'After all these years? I suppose he expects me to be glad he's finally remembered I exist!'

'It's not like that.' Cal was completely lost. At his feet Sears took advantage of this distraction and rose to his knees. When Cal didn't try to stop him he stood up, watching from under half-closed lids again. The man was halfway to the door before Cal grabbed him and pulled him back.

'You can hold on,' Cal said. 'We'll get to you in a minute.' He pushed Sears into the chair Eliza Prentice had vacated.

'I don't see why he sent you,' she said. 'If you're going to tell me he's here in town, expecting me to welcome him with open arms once you've broken the news—'

'I wish I was,' Cal said sincerely. 'Ma'am, miss, Shorty wasn't so bad, I swear. He thought he'd done the best he could by you, and by your mother too, I reckon. When she died he thought you'd ended up with a good God-fearing family, and he didn't want to mess up your life. Coming back was about the last thing he'd do, seeing what he was. Look, I'm making a real bad job here. Fact is, I came to give you this.' And he reached into his pocket for the crumpled letter.

The whiskey went down on top of the beer, smooth and with a good kick. It was the first in a long time, and Cal made the most of it. He leant on the bar and signalled for a refill, counting out coins. He was pleased with himself, and figured he deserved another drink, even if it meant he'd be short of supplies on the journey north. Anyway, once he'd put a few hundred miles between him and Macomber he'd maybe stop for a while. He'd find work and earn enough to see him to Canada.

He took his time over the second shot of whiskey. Sears had followed his orders like a well-trained hound dog, except that he'd resolutely refused to go in the store and buy a woman's dress. Finally Cal had gone in alone and chosen a simple calico outfit that looked about the right size for the girl. Then a while later he'd stood and watched from a distance as Sears escorted her to the bank.

This was a changed Eliza, her face scrubbed clean of tears, the black bandanna exchanged for a blue one. When they came out of the bank she was carrying a small package. She turned away from Sears without a look or a word, to enter another shop further down the street, though she paused long enough to give Cal a little wave and a smile before she disappeared inside.

There wasn't much left in the glass. Cal took a sip and thought about buying a bottle, but if he did then he'd have nothing but jerky to eat, and not a lot of that. What was it Moke had said? Whiskey and women, that was what he missed when he was on the run. And he'd said a man could have too much of either one, though he sure didn't want to make do with too little.

Eliza Prentice was a real pretty woman. No, she was downright beautiful. Cal sighed, trying to recall when he'd last spent time with a girl who could make a man's heart beat faster, and have him wishing he'd got something smarter to put on than a cheap check shirt. There had been no one, not since Hope Macomber turned him down three years since, to marry Mort Bailey instead.

That had been a bad time. Before Bailey's wife died in an accident, Hope had been promised to Cal, they'd been walking out together for a couple of years. There were plenty of uncharitable souls who said Mort Bailey didn't love the Macomber girl, and that he'd only wanted a mother for his eight-year-old son, Joe, or that he'd married her to ingratiate himself with her brother Glenn, who was Bannack County's sheriff. There were even some who'd wondered out loud whether he'd simply stolen Cal Mason's girl out of spite.

As the seasons turned, Cal got used to Hope's change of

mind. He'd even been glad; within a year she was just like Mort, obsessed with money and her position among the townsfolk. She no longer had time for the simple pleasures she seemed to enjoy when Cal was courting her; she was never seen walking now she had a handsome buggy to ride in.

'Mason?' A hand landed heavily on his arm and Cal spun around to find himself staring into a pair of piercing grey eyes. Below a bulbous nose, a greying moustache decorated a mouth that right now was twisted into a sardonic smile. 'You must be some kind of a fool.'

The man matched him for height, but carried twice as much weight. On the breast of the plain yellow waistcoat that stretched tight across his chest was a fancy star with the word 'Sheriff' emblazoned upon it. In a split second Cal considered a dozen options, coming up with nothing useful, unless he wanted to commit murder in front of a dozen witnesses.

'Sheriff?' he croaked, pretending that a mouthful of whiskey had gone the wrong way and coughing long and loud.

The man laughed. 'Well, I sure am sorry, didn't mean to make you jump that way. But I reckon any man who leaves a lovely lady waiting in the sun for half an hour needs his head examined.'

Cal looked at him blankly, his heartbeat thundering in his ears. He swallowed hard. 'A lady?'

'Yeah. Mind you, she says half an hour, an' I know for a fact it wasn't more'n five minutes, because I watched her walk up the street. Still, she says she's been kept waiting, and I figure that counts as a crime. Seeing as I'm not in the mood to go arresting anyone just now, you'd best get on out there an' smooth things over.'

'I'll do that,' Cal said, tipping the last of his drink down his throat and feeling as if it would take several more to bring his racing pulse back to normal. 'I'm obliged to you.'

'No trouble,' the sheriff smiled and beckoned to the barman. 'Since I'm here I reckon I'll have a beer.'

With a nod Cal made for the way out, somehow managing to take it slow, and trying to ignore the prickle between his shoulder blades. Was the lawman watching him? As he pushed through the swing doors he let out a long breath. For a moment there he had almost felt the noose tightening around his neck; the sooner he got started for Canada the better.

He stepped out into the daylight and came to a dead halt. A lady, the sheriff had said. Since Cal had no other acquaintances in Kentville, Cal had expected to see Shorty Prentice's daughter.

Her bright blonde hair was pulled back from the sides of her face, yet it gave the impression of being a mass of curls. The outfit this woman wore was a million miles away from the simple calico he'd bought for Eliza, yet it was simple and practical, a wealthy lady's travelling suit with a split skirt. On her head was a jaunty hat, with just enough of a brim to keep the sun out of her eyes.

She turned at the sound of the door swinging shut behind him, and he let out a long low whistle. The transformation was unbelievable, but there was no mistake. This was the girl he'd seen only a few hours ago, dressed in rags and close to tears because she thought she'd killed a man.

'Jeez!' The word escaped before he could stop it. 'Sorry,

ma'am, I mean Miss Prentice. You kind of took my breath away.'

She smiled at him, radiant with pleasure, and instantly became herself again. 'Thank you, Mr Mason. I believe I'll take that as a compliment. I'm not used to looking like this. I felt uncomfortable standing outside a saloon, so I hope you'll forgive me for sending somebody to fetch you.'

'Sure, though I wish you hadn't chosen the sheriff. Gave me a bad moment there, when it turned out he knew my name.'

Her hands flew to her mouth in a gesture he was already coming to recognize. 'Oh, I didn't think. Of course, you were a friend of my father's. I'm so sorry. I hope. . . .'

'It's fine, my heartbeat's just about back to normal. Look, if you want to talk maybe we should go somewhere a bit more private.'

'Where?' She looked around. 'I can't go back to the Sears house.'

'No. I was thinking of the hotel.' He took hold of her arm. 'They'll maybe have a room that's suitable for a lady to sit down in when she wants to talk, though I doubt they'll approve of me.'

Her eyes sparkled. 'Could we have some tea?' she asked, suddenly childlike. 'When I was a little girl my mother used to take me to the hotel for tea sometimes, as a treat.'

Cal hesitated for no more than a moment. He didn't know how much tea cost, but he hadn't the heart to refuse her. The internal sigh at the thought of several more days on short rations didn't reach his lips and he nodded. 'Tea. That'll be just dandy.'

*

'I wanted to say thank you,' Eliza said, looking at him solemnly across the little table. 'I don't know what might have happened if you hadn't arrived when you did.'

'You'd have thought of something,' Cal assured her.

'Maybe.' She was silent for a while. 'Do you know what was in my father's letter?'

'No, ma'am.'

'I thought not.' She took the crumpled sheet from the elegant little reticule she carried. 'I'd like you to read it, if you don't mind.' She noticed his hesitation and flushed. 'Oh, I mean, you can read? I'm sorry. . . .'

'I can,' Cal said, reluctantly taking the paper, 'Though I'm not sure I should. He addressed it to you.'

'Please.'

Cal skipped over the greeting and the brief references to her childhood. As he scanned the next part he looked up at her sharply. 'You've done what he says?'

She nodded. 'I've seen the deeds. The bank will keep them for me, but the land will become mine as soon as the formalities are done. You know, I don't remember that place at all; we left when I was a baby. I used to ask my mother to take me there, but she refused even to talk about it.'

'Guess that's not so strange,' Cal said, 'seeing what happened there.'

'My brother. Yes. I'm afraid I don't remember him either.' She stared down at her hands for a moment. 'I know I don't have any right, when you've already done so much, but I need you to help me some more. You see, in order for the land to become mine, there has to be proof that my father is no longer alive, other than his letter.'

Cal grimaced. It was quite a few weeks since he'd buried Shorty's body. He doubted if he'd be able to find the grave, and even if he did, the dead man might not be too recognizable by now.

'I told them you'd seen him,' she said, as if she'd read his thoughts. 'The lawyer is going to draw up the proper documents. If you're prepared to sign a paper then I believe that will do.' She made patterns on the table with her fingers. 'I suppose you must think I'm very hard-hearted, talking about it this way, but I can barely remember him. And so much has happened today, none of this seems quite real.'

'I guess not.' Cal chewed on his lip. 'Guess I need to do some explaining too. I don't want to stay in town too long. Something might jog the sheriff's memory.'

'You mean he might have heard your name? In connection with. . . .' she faltered.

Without a word Cal took the handbill from his pocket, glancing around to see there was nobody near. He shook the paper open and showed it to her.

'Oh.' Her fingers fluttered to her mouth. She studied the picture before looking earnestly at his face. There was a faint glow of pink on her cheeks as she spoke again. 'It doesn't look much like you.'

'Is that all you've got to say?' Cal asked, tucking the handbill back out of sight. 'You're taking tea with a murderer.'

The blush deepened and she lowered her eyes. 'Please, read the rest of the letter.'

There wasn't much more, except the part where Shorty mentioned his name. He wrote that Cal Mason was more honest than most of the men he'd met in the years since he'd last seen Eliza, and if she needed help then Cal would be a good man to ask.

With a slight frown he handed the letter back. 'I'll come and sign a paper to say I buried your father,' he said. 'Once that's done you won't need me any more.'

'No, though I—' she began.

'You could find yourself a respectable job,' Cal broke in quickly. 'You'd look real elegant in a ladies' store. With the money you got from Sears you can go wherever you want.'

'I know. But there's only one place I want to go.' She turned deep-blue eyes on him. 'My father left me his ranch, Mr. Mason. I haven't been there since I was a small child, and I want to see it again. Please, will you take me?'

CHAPTER SEVEN

'No,' Cal said, for the tenth time at least. 'There are men up there in your father's cabin, the kind of men you don't want to meet.' He gave her lovely oval face a long searching look, then let his eyes travel down over her trim frame, dwelling for a while on her most alluring attractions, not hiding the way she made him feel.

'Mr Mason,' she protested, looking very young as her cheeks flushed bright red.

'I'm sorry,' he said. 'You don't care to be looked at that way. No decent woman does. But you need to take my word on this. The men I'm talking about are a whole lot worse than Sears. They wouldn't settle for just looking. You couldn't deal with the Hinds gang by flattening them with a pan.'

That brought a half smile to her lips but she wouldn't be side-tracked. 'I'd be willing to pay,' she said. 'I already decided. Two hundred dollars. And if you won't do it,' she added defiantly, before he had time to refuse yet again, 'then I'll find somebody who will.'

'Nobody'd be fool enough to take up an offer like that while there's a gang of outlaws hiding out in that cabin,' Cal said, 'not for ten times that amount. You might find some man who'll agree to take you, but he'll steal your money and leave you out in the wilds someplace. Or worse.'

'I'm not a child, Mr Mason, I think I know the risks.'

He leant across the little table, dropping his voice a little. 'Miss Prentice, you may not have had an easy life these last few years, but you've sure had a sheltered one. There's a lot of men who'll disrespect a woman once they've got her alone. You have to be sensible, there are times when the only way out of trouble is to avoid it in the first place.'

There was a stubborn look on her face and he knew she wasn't convinced. Cal shook his head. 'Ma'am, believe me, I know a whole lot more about the ways of the world than you do. Besides, there won't always be a cooking pot ready and waiting when you need it.'

This time she laughed outright. 'Maybe I should buy one and keep it handy. In fact, it's a shame I left that pan behind. Since everything else has failed perhaps I could have tried it on you.'

'Never found anything that'd knock any sense into my head,' Cal told her, 'but if you won't listen to me, try asking the sheriff. Though not while I'm still around,' he added hastily.

She looked at him solemnly for a moment then rose from her chair. 'Thank you for the tea. I think it's time we went to see Mr Hughes.'

'Please,' he said, coming to his feet as she did, suddenly deadly serious. 'Promise you won't try anything stupid. That ranch is no place for you.'

'All right, if I can't go to the valley why don't you go for me? Those men can't stay there forever. You told me you

like it there. Why not take care of the cabin for me, until
it's safe for me to visit?'

Cal sighed. If only he'd headed north instead of going
into the saloon. He'd have been miles away by now, on his
way to Canada.

They sat in silence in the lawyer's office. Finally the grey-
faced man on the other side of the desk lifted his head. 'I
believe we have all the relevant details,' he said. 'I shall
have the papers ready for you to sign on Thursday. Shall
we say two-thirty in the afternoon?'

'You want me back here on Thursday?' Cal shook his
head. 'I got places to go.'

The man looked down his nose at him and sniffed, his
gaze settling for a few seconds on Cal's battered hat, looking out of place on the corner of his highly polished desk.
'If it is a question of finance I believe it would be proper
for Miss Prentice to offer you a retainer.'

Cal scowled. 'I told you, I've got other places to be.'

'This property could be quite valuable in the future,'
Hughes said drily, 'should Miss Prentice wish to sell. I
would suggest a fee of ten dollars, half to be paid now, the
rest when you make yourself available on Thursday.'

'I'm not after her money,' Cal said. 'I just don't fancy
hanging around that long.'

The lawyer looked at him in disbelief, and Cal tried to
think up some good reason to refuse to stay, other than
the truth. He didn't want to hang around in any town
where the sheriff knew his name and had already taken a
good look at his face.

Eliza was delving in the little reticule she carried, bringing out a large bundle of bills. She peeled some off and

offered them to him. 'Ten doesn't seem much,' she said. 'You'll need a place to sleep. Here's twenty. You can have it all now. And you don't have to stay in town the whole time, if . . . if you have other business to attend to. Just as long as you're here on Thursday, like Mr Hughes says.'

Hughes' dry cough suggested he didn't approve of this generosity, but Eliza ignored him. 'Well, Mr Mason?' she prompted. There was fear lingering at the back of her eyes, but she was trying to smile. 'If you refuse then I might not be able to claim the ranch. I don't want to go back to work for Mr and Mrs Sears.'

Cal shook his head. 'You won't.' She was so beautiful, she didn't need to worry; every unmarried man in town would be begging to let him take her up the aisle. There wasn't much of Shorty in this girl, except perhaps his courage, though that had failed him in the end. Cal sighed. His friend would want him to see this through, and if he wasn't there on Thursday this stuffed shirt might make difficulties. Even though nobody would pay a bent nickel for the valley right now, this country was opening up; Kentville was a thriving town, and those who didn't respect the law were gradually being driven further into the badlands. If she hung on to that land for a few years Eliza Prentice could be a rich woman.

'You got a deal,' Cal said, grimacing as he took the money. At least it meant he'd be able to eat. And he assured himself that by four o'clock on Thursday he'd be hightailing it out of town and on his way to Canada.

With Eliza settled into the hotel, which was the only respectable place in town where a single lady could stay and preserve her reputation, Cal found himself a room at the back of the Golden Nugget. At her insistence he returned to the hotel so they could have dinner together. She wanted to pay for the meal, and was digging in her heels until Cal asked quietly if he should go to the kitchen and ask to borrow a frying pan, at which she blushed furiously and allowed him to pay without further argument.

'What will you do?' Eliza asked, as he rose to leave.

'Ma'am?' he asked. 'I said I'd be here Thursday. Then I'll be leaving.'

'But that's two days away.' She was blushing again, and staring down at the tablecloth. 'I know you won't take me to the valley, but I thought perhaps. . . .' She looked up at him, and the defiant light he'd seen in her eyes when she tackled Sears was back. 'I know it's not the kind of thing a lady should do, asking. . . .' Her voice trailed away to nothing, and she stared at him in mute appeal.

'Miss Prentice, ma'am,' Cal said, feeling a heat rising in his own face, and suddenly very preoccupied with his battered hat, which he was twisting in his hands. 'Would you by any chance be suggesting we might spend a little time together tomorrow? Because if that's it, I reckon I'd be real honoured.'

With that the smile returned and her eyes sparkled. 'Why, Mr Mason, what a very fine idea. And how kind of you to ask me. What do you think it might be proper for a lady and a gentleman to do?'

'I could hire a buggy,' Cal said, 'if you'd care to go for a drive. On the way into town I noticed a fine shady place down by the river.'

With a time and place agreed on for their meeting next day, Cal bade her a polite good night and headed out onto the street.

In the Golden Nugget the customers were settling

down to the serious business of the evening; those interested in drinking were propping up the bar, while several tables had been set up for the gamblers intent on losing their money at poker or faro. Cal didn't mean to do either, heading straight for the door at the back, but a voice hailed him.

'Hey, Mr Mason, ain't it?' It was the sheriff. He stood at the bar, a bottle in front of him. 'I didn't get the chance to introduce myself properly when we met before. My name's Bradbury. Folks call me J. T. Why don't you join me for a drink?' He reached over the counter for another glass, and poured a shot of whiskey, handing it to Cal.

'Thanks,' Cal said shortly, tossing most of the drink off in one.

'That's a real pretty girl you've been escorting around town,' Sheriff Bradbury said. 'An' there's a few rumours flying around about how Shorty Prentice's daughter came to leave the Sears house and turn herself into a lady. Some say you had a hand in that. Some say the money that bought her pretty new outfit might not have been come by honest, seeing as how her father had a price on his head.'

Cal stared at the whiskey in his glass. 'The money came from Sears,' he said.

'Is that so? Makes a man wonder why an old skinflint like Sears suddenly got all generous that way, and why the girl takes up with a stranger who's only just ridden into town.' Bradbury's eyes narrowed as he studied Cal's face. 'But maybe you ain't such a stranger. I'm sure I know you from somewhere.'

'Mason's a pretty common name.'

The sheriff shook his head. 'It's not the name, it's the face that's familiar. Were you ever in Laramie?'

'No. And if you're working around to asking if I knew Shorty Prentice then the answer's yes, we rode together for a while. He told me he'd been on the wrong side of the law a time or two. Can't say we were friends exactly, but when he died I buried him, decent as I could.' Cal drained his glass. 'He left a letter for his daughter. Least I could do was bring it to her. I walked in on Sears when he was trying to take advantage of the girl, figured I had to help her out. Far as I know I didn't break any laws.'

Bradbury went on looking at him. 'No?'

No.' Cal said. 'You're a mighty persistent man, Sheriff. Fact is, I told Sears it was time he paid for all the years of work him and his wife beat out of that girl. He agreed, seeing I could have come to your office and backed her up when she accused him of trying to rape her. Sears didn't think Mrs Sears would like that.'

'Don't reckon she would at that,' Bradbury agreed, nodding, a more friendly light in his eyes.

'Thanks for the drink. Think I'll turn in.' Cal put the glass down. 'Unless there's anything else you want to know, Sheriff?'

Bradbury smiled. 'Don't reckon there is. Not right now. 'Night.'

Cal headed for the door leading to the bedrooms, sure he could feel the sheriff's eyes following him every step of the way.

The valley lay silent in the evening sun, long shadows stretching away from the cabin and the fence around the corral. Cal led the black into the barn. He came back out a few minutes later, stretching, staring at the waving grass and away to the distant mountains. It was a beautiful place, and now that Dobey Hinds and the Rodway brothers were gone he could picture it as a working ranch, as Shorty and his wife must have known it. He turned towards the cabin, and for a fleeting instant he imagined Eliza Prentice standing in the doorway, smiling as she welcomed him home for his supper.

Angrily Cal swept his hat off his head, chasing the dream away. He'd been thinking a deal too much about that woman. As he lit the stove and put the coffee pot on to boil he remembered that this was the day he was supposed to be in Silverlode to meet the Hinds gang. They were planning to rob the bank, tonight perhaps, or in the morning. And in a few days they'd be back at the cabin. What in tarnation was he doing here? Why had he let Eliza persuade him? It wasn't as if he'd ever dare to ride back to Kentville, not with Sheriff J. T. Bradbury watching his every move.

Next day Cal rode out early, exploring the rolling grasslands, heading up into the higher ground, going as far as he could before the enclosing hills turned him back. He followed the river, sluggish and shallow as it waited for the rains, tracing it down until he found the place where it vanished into a great chasm in the ground, tipping over with a grumbling murmur that would be a deafening roar when the water was high. It must resurface somewhere far out on the plain; all the surrounding prairie was dry. Again his mind wandered, and he was back with Eliza by the river, strolling under the trees.

They had taken a buggy and driven out of town. He could see her now, that silly hat tipped forward over her face. He'd loved the way she laughed when he tried to straighten it. The longing to kiss her at that moment had been so strong, he still didn't know how he'd resisted. He had wanted to take her in his arms, to feel her warm softness against his body. . . .

Cal spurred the black savagely, driving it to a wild gallop. It had been a mistake coming back here, he should have headed for Canada as soon as he left Kentville. Reaching the cabin he turned the horse loose in the corral and fetched a mattock, starting to clear the patch that had once been Shorty's vegetable plot. He worked fast, the dust from the hard ground billowing up to cling to his sweat-streaked body and coat his throat so he was constantly parched, no matter how often he went to drink from the well.

His heart pounded and his muscles ached, but he couldn't drive the image of Eliza Prentice from his mind. Darkness fell. He'd eaten nothing since morning. At last he staggered back into the cabin. Throwing himself down on his bedroll he fell instantly asleep, but dreams of Eliza troubled him all through the night.

CHAPTER EIGHT

Cal brushed sweat out of his eyes. The new fence was coming along well; he'd soon have a bigger corral for the horses. He'd been alone in the valley for three days now, and he never wanted to leave.

Except to go back to Kentville – for Eliza, and a visit with her to the parson. The trouble was, he was afraid maybe she'd changed her mind about him by now. There'd be plenty of men wanting to court her, and every one of them with far more to offer than an outlaw on the run. He was basing his future hopes, his whole life, on dreams he'd built out of the memory of the two days they'd spent together. Cal sighed, lifted the second rail into place against the post and started knocking another nail in.

In the next instant the world went crazy. There was blackness, then a spray of red before his eyes. He was suddenly flat on his back. The blow to his head had been so unexpected that he didn't realize what had happened right away, then he recalled hearing the unmistakable crack of a rifle shot as he'd fallen. Putting a hand to his head, he felt the warm wetness of blood. Then the pain began.

There was a familiar sound that prodded Cal into action. Somebody was pulling back the thorn barrier! On knees and elbows he propelled himself to the water trough where he'd left his rifle. His left eye was blind, but if he blinked frequently he could still see out of the right, though the effort made his head ache so bad he thought he might pass out. It was tempting, to let himself sink into oblivion, to be free of the pain ... something told him that was a bad idea.

With the Henry in his hand Cal dived into the narrow space alongside the wood stack, twisting as he landed, so he could see the barrier. A man was coming through, short, bowlegged, with another following, much bigger. Both wore clothes covered in trail dust and had unshaven faces, both wore six-guns tied down on their thighs, both carried rifles held ready as they scanned the dusty yard.

He had to move, and fast. There was a little pool of blood under his head. Cal clasped his left hand to his forehead, rose to his feet and went at a fast crouching run across to the barn, expecting a bullet to find him at every second. Then he was inside, hidden by the cool darkness, but he knew the feeling of safety was an illusion.

He had recognized the big man. Hambo, so called because of his fat face and snout-like nose, had been one of the men who got away when Glenn Macomber captured Wally Yeldon. And the guy with him must be his sidekick, Titch Wilkie, wanted for murdering two passengers on a stagecoach, one of them a woman.

'You sure he ain't one of Dobey's gang?' Wilkie called, his voice carrying in the still hot air so Cal could hear him quite clearly.

There was the sound of somebody kicking the saw Cal

had been using, and scattering his pot of nails. 'Hinds must have moved on. This fella's a damnfool dirt farmer.' Hambo laughed. 'Maybe Shorty Prentice sold the place! Who gives a damn, let's finish him.'

They would be moving, trying to get round either side of the barn and cut off Cal's only escape route. He ran, out through the back door and into the feed store. There were some rotting planks in the far wall he hadn't gotten round to fixing. He squeezed out, slapped his hand over the wound in his head again in the hopes that he could prevent any telltale drops of blood from leaving a trail. In these days alone he'd learnt many of the valley's secrets. There was a cave in the rocks not far from the cabin, the entrance a narrow slit just wide enough for a man to slither through.

Inside the cave Cal watched and waited, trying vainly to keep the blood out of his right eye; without sight he was a dead man. The two intruders had been through the cabin, now they were searching the barn. He heard one of them cursing when a board in the loft gave way underfoot. They moved on to the feed store.

A drumbeat was echoing in Cal's head, pounding in time with the pain that pulsed behind his eyes. If he moved he felt instantly dizzy, so he stayed still, on his knees, the rifle jammed into his shoulder and aimed at the open ground between him and the cabin. In time they had to come. Blood oozed constantly down his face and he wondered how long it would take a man to bleed to death.

There was a shout of triumph. They'd found the trail of damp dark droplets in the feed store. Wilkie, small enough to follow where Cal had gone, was squeezing out through the gap in the wall. Hambo would be slower, having to go back through the barn.

Cal's breathing was ragged now, and there was a mist across his one good eye. Wilkie was coming, tracking him, head turning slowly as he searched for possible hiding places. But it was no good taking on just one of them, he would get no second chance. At last Hambo appeared, walking slow, scanning the back of the cabin, then glancing at the ground as if looking for more bloodstains. One step nearer, two, three. . . .

Biting his lip, struggling to remain conscious just a little longer, Cal drew a bead on Wilkie's chest. The man dropped, not making a sound, just folding up like a puppet with its strings cut. With his head spinning, and a great roaring in his ears, Cal swivelled to turn the gun on Hambo.

He was cold, lying on a river of ice. No, he was in it, buried deep in the frozen water. It was strange, he thought idly, that the ice was moving, sweeping him along; rivers moved, but not when they were frozen. Soon he would reach that great drop where the water disappeared underground, tipping over the edge to fall into the dark.

It came as a surprise to realize he wasn't alone; somebody was doing their best to hammer a hole in the ice, only they kept hitting his head instead. He wanted to be free, to escape before the ice trapped him forever beneath the foothills, but the hammer blows hurt too much; above all else he wanted them to stop.

Cal moaned, and the sound of his own voice brought him closer to consciousness. He moved a hand, surprised to find that he could. The ice must be melting. Yet he felt no warmer; he was shivering. He thought he opened his eyes, but he saw nothing but blackness. For a long time he lay there, blind, cold, the thudding blows sometimes originating inside his head, and sometimes inflicted by a man. Cal couldn't see him, yet he knew he was a pig-faced brute, big and ugly. In time the pickaxe would break through Cal's skull, and perhaps then his tormentor would be sastisfied.

Redness. His first clear thought was that it made a change from black. He moved his hand to his face and felt the hard crust of dried blood. Wanting to wipe it away he put his fingers to his mouth, but there was no wetness there, his tongue was bone dry and swollen. He picked at the blood with his fingernails, barely noticing when they scratched the skin, and at last his right eye opened.

The early morning sun was shining in through the narrow entrance to the cave. It had been that, warming the top of his head and his outstretched hand, that had driven away the ice and brought him back to life.

How long it took Cal to crawl out of the cave and across to the well he never knew. By the time he had drunk his fill, cleaned his face and found that his left eye hadn't been damaged, just filled with blood from the wound, the sun was high in the sky. A sticky warm wetness was oozing down his face again. Staggering dizzily into the cabin he looked about him for a bandage. The cleanest cloth he could find was the shirt he'd bought in Kentville, and he bound it awkwardly over the wound. Cal sank into the chair, folded his arms before him on the table and laid his head on them.

As the sun dipped towards the west he came to again, and this time he knew who and where he was. He went out to look for the two men he'd killed. Wilkie lay where he'd dropped, dead before he hit the ground. Hambo hadn't been so lucky. The shot Cal couldn't remember firing had taken the man in the belly, and he'd died slow. An ugly trail of blood and guts led towards the cave entrance. Cal hadn't even noticed the body that morning, but Hambo had been only four yards from his hiding place when he died, a loaded rifle in one hand, the fingers of the other curled into a claw as they clutched at the dusty ground.

Cal found two horses out beyond the thorn barrier. He led them through and left them to drink their fill at the water trough, while he took the length of rope that hung on one saddle and returned to Titch Wilkie's body. It was beyond his strength to lift even this small man, but he dragged him across to lie beside his dead partner. He tied the two together, wrapping a bedroll off the saddle around the ungainly bundle, then hitched the other end of the rope to the saddlebow. Somehow he hoisted himself onto the second horse's back.

The animals balked, hating the smell of death, but Cal forced them up the valley, dragging the grizzly load, until he reached the rocky ground below the mountains. He cast the rope off; there were scavengers here, they would do a better job of disposing of the two carcasses than he could manage.

He lost count of time; whole days must have passed but he didn't remember. Sometimes he thought vaguely about the Hinds gang, wondering where they were. For a while he got them confused with Wilkie and Hambo, and suspected he'd killed them. He tended the three horses, often forgetting where the two extra ones had come from, surprised to find the black no longer alone when he went into the barn. There was a patch of white hair growing over a scar on the black's neck. He couldn't recall how it got there.

He talked to the horses, missing the people who had once been in the cabin – a man with a white moustache, another with odd quicksilver eyes who'd spoken about whiskey and women. And hadn't there been a girl? No, that had to be a dream; no woman would be up here in the wilds. Maybe he was going mad. Once he heard a man's voice, quite clear in his head, although he was alone. 'There's times he acts real foolish, some folks say he's just plumb crazy. . . .' Had the words referred to him? Thinking hurt, and he didn't try it often. Occasionally he remembered to eat.

Then one day he woke to find that the pain in his head had eased, and he was hungry. After that the world started to make a little sense again and his memory began to return. The cabin was in chaos, precious coffee beans scattered in the doorway, a bucket of grain on the table, half eaten strips of jerky lying on the floor.

Cal cooked a mess of beans and brewed coffee for breakfast, tidied up some, then stepped out into the sunlight. The half-built fence was just as he'd left it, except that the saw lay several yards away, and the nails had been scattered. He picked them up, but made no attempt to finish the job. Instead he took his rifle, saddled the black and rode up to the lookout.

If the raid on the bank had been successful he supposed Hinds would be back. He wasn't sure what he'd do then. Dreams of Eliza Prentice still troubled him; he'd met her in Kentville, he knew, but there were gaps in his memory. In the end he decided most of what had appar-

74

ently happened between them was a fantasy; the bullet that had creased his skull had put a great distance between him and everything that happened before he came to this place.

Later, as he cooked his meal, Cal found himself staring at the big black stove, and wondered why he'd never thought about it before; Shorty couldn't possibly have brought that thing along the ridge, it was far too heavy for one animal to carry. And there'd been cattle, a story of how Shorty had taken steers to Silverlode each year. Unlikely as it seemed, there had to be another way into the valley, one where there'd be no danger of a herd falling hundreds of feet off a cliff.

Next day Cal rode to the lookout again and kept watch for a while, then he began his search for the hidden road, working his way methodically around the edge of the valley, riding up every gorge and canyon, exploring any slope that wasn't too steep for horses. He returned to the lookout before the light failed, scanning the horizon for telltale clouds of dust. His memory still had gaps in it, but he expected the Hinds gang to turn up sometime, and some instinct told him others could come that way too. He'd found the wanted poster in his pocket, and guessed a posse might come looking for him.

It took him four days to find the way out of the valley. Hidden from view behind an outcrop of rock was what looked like a blind canyon, but bedded deep in the blown dirt at the junction was a wagon wheel. The narrow gorge twisted, and as he turned the corner Cal drew in a sharp intake of breath. He was high above the prairie, on a wide level shelf of grass. The old road was still visible, slanting across the hillside. He followed it for a while. Looking

75

back, he discovered that this end of the trail was even harder to find than the other. Going almost down to level ground he was satisfied he could find his way into the valley from below, then he turned and headed home.

Cal was in the lookout two days later when the plume of dust appeared, far off towards Kentville. It would take more than three horses to throw up that amount of dirt, so it wasn't likely to be the Hinds gang. Cal watched through the old telescope, seeing the shapes gradually emerge from the heat haze and turn into figures on horseback. He counted eight riders. They were travelling at a steady lope, purposeful but not in any great hurry.

There was just a chance the men were on their way north, riding up the trail with business of their own. But they slowed as they reached the opening in the foothills, the one marked by the corresponding notch in the mountains. Cal blinked, staring into the eyepiece until his eyes watered. As they milled briefly, gathering round a man on a tall roan horse, he knew for sure that this was a posse, and they were looking for him.

The man on the roan was Glenn Macomber, Sheriff of Bannack County. Glenn Macomber, the brother-in-law of the man he'd killed. Glenn Macomber, once his best friend. How could he have forgotten? Cal put his hand to his forehead, feeling the rough half-healed line of raised flesh. He lifted the telescope and looked again. Beside Macomber was another man he thought he knew. Flashes of memory returned. A day of relentless heat. The weight of the youngster's body on his back as he toiled along the ridge, and a horse lying dead in the gully.

CHAPTER NINE

Cal's first instinct was to run, to head for Shorty's old road through the hidden canyon. Eventually Macomber and his men would ride into the valley; finding the cabin undefended they would think he'd ridden out across the ridge days before. By the time the posse picked up the trail it would be cold, and with the two horses he'd got from Hambo and Wilkie he'd easily outrun them.

Trouble was he didn't want to leave. The valley felt like home. And there was Eliza; despite his loss of memory he had an idea she'd wanted him to stay, that she'd planned to come back here one day. That he might figure in her plans for the future was too much for Cal to hope for; he still couldn't sort out the dreams from the reality; had they really shared a buggy ride? The bullet that creased his skull had made him pretty crazy for a while. Maybe his memory of that walk by the river was just an illusion.

It wasn't a good time to think about Eliza; he had the posse to worry about. One memory was still clear; he could see the smoking gun in his hand as he looked down at Mort Bailey's body. And he'd found the crumpled handbill in his pocket. Glenn Macomber had been his friend, yet he'd put a price on his head.

Cal tried to fill in the great gaps in his past. He remembered how he'd encountered Seth Bailey. He couldn't recall how their meeting ended, but something told him it was important. Bailey had sure been eager to catch him, that much he knew, and now the kid had returned still limping, barely recovered from that broken leg, so it looked like he was just as keen on earning himself that reward. And yet for some reason Cal had never expected to see young Bailey again. What had given him that idea?

As the night closed in around him Cal stayed at the lookout, only half his mind on the men intent on dragging him back to Bannack County. Fingering the scar on his forehead he sighed. What had the youngster said to him that he couldn't recall? Or had it been the other way around? Had he told the kid something important? He stared into the darkness, but nothing new came to him, only half remembered glimpses of that day, the heat and exhaustion, an injured kid lying under a dead horse. At last, convinced that the posse wouldn't make a move that night, he slithered down to where the black waited and headed back to the cabin.

As he dismounted by the barn, another of Cal's feverish dreams came to him; he'd seen Eliza waiting for him at the cabin door. She'd been smiling at him, opening her arms in welcome. Cal grimaced. Maybe nothing he thought they'd shared was real; by now the girl was probably on a stage heading for Silverlode. Like as not he'd never see her again. Leaving a horse saddled in case he needed to leave in a hurry, Cal fixed some food then turned in. Sleep was a long time coming.

Cal was back in the lookout at first light. The posse were scattered around the camp and he counted, relieved to see there were still eight horses, although after several minutes he had seen only seven men, which worried him some.

There was a makeshift tent set back a few feet from the

fire, a couple of sheets of canvas propped up, with stones holding down the sides. He couldn't figure what it was for, until somebody came out from beneath its shadow, straightening up to put on a wide brimmed hat. Cal's heart leapt. She wore pants and a loose-fitting shirt, not the fancy travelling outfit she'd worn for their buggy ride, and the bright blonde curls were tucked up and tied back, but there was no mistaking Eliza.

Cal scowled as he stared through the telescope, seeing her smile at a man seated by the fire, biting his lip when he saw who it was. This was the girl he'd rescued from Sears. Maybe she didn't love him, but hadn't she been grateful for his help? Yet here she was, camped out with Glenn Macomber, the man who wanted to take him back to Bannack county and string him up.

The sound of the shot echoed from the hills. Men scattered. Cal fired the Henry for a second time, slapping a bullet into the ground in front of a bandy-legged man who'd been slow in running for cover; he made up for it now, scooting out of sight.

Without pausing for breath Cal leapt down to a lower shelf of rock, jumping across a narrow crevasse to reach the slit in the rocks where he'd propped the scattergun. He'd found the weapon in the cabin, left behind by the Hinds gang when they rode to Silverlode.

The scattergun was loaded and ready, and Cal took the shot without bothering to aim, intent only on convincing the posse that the trail was well guarded. He didn't think Glenn Macomber was going to be fooled much longer, and when the sheriff figured out he was up against just one man he'd be coming through the gulch with everything he'd got.

Sweat pouring off him, Cal scrambled back up the slope and snatched up his rifle for another quick shot, aiming at a man who'd squashed up against the cliffs. A spray of dust lifted from the ground as the slug missed by inches. After that he was no longer in such a hurry, and he took his time. A telltale patch of red cloth, bright in the sunlight, showed where another member of the posse had hidden himself in a shallow arroyo. Cal took aim with great care, grinning when the bullet shaved a sliver of rock off the man's hiding place. When the dust cleared the scrap of red had gone.

Cal was tired. He'd stayed at his post through a whole day and night, expecting an attack after sunset. While the moon was high the posse could easily have followed the trail to the ridge, but they must have feared an ambush, and they'd waited until the darkest hour to try and find their way in. He'd heard them moving down below him and fired a couple of warning shots, aiming high for fear of hitting Eliza, though common sense told him Macomber would keep the girl out of range. Pausing between shots, once the echo had died away Cal heard a man yell from the opposite side of the gulch. There was a curse quickly cut off and a rattle of stone, followed by a confused babble of voices. A while later the men scrambled back out of the canyon, abandoning the assault.

It had been a relief to see Eliza soon after dawn, on her knees by the fire. Cal tried to figure out why she was there; maybe she thought Macomber could rid her valley of outlaws, not caring that Cal was one of them. The sight of her sent his pulse racing. Even if she'd betrayed him, the way he felt wouldn't change; it was something he couldn't control, as natural as breathing.

The morning light had brought this new attack, but

he'd halted their dash for the gorge, and he'd got them pegged down. There was a shout. As one, the three men emerged from their bolt holes. Cal put the Henry to his shoulder, but the posse was in retreat. He let them go. At that range he didn't trust his aim, and he hadn't sunk low enough to put a bullet in a man's back.

Macomber would be getting mad at being held up so long, Cal figured, as he slithered down to reload the shot-gun, though he didn't think the sheriff would try another night attack; one man was hobbling around with the help of a couple of sticks, while another sat by the fire with a bandage round his head. Cal was pretty sure he hadn't shot either one of them.

As the day grew hot Macomber and his men gathered around the camp-fire, drinking coffee, maybe trying to figure out what to do next. Soon they would launch another attack and if they came in strength Cal would stand no chance.

He chewed on cold deer meat, and drank from one of his canteens; he would have to return to the cabin for supplies, but not yet. Once his meal was finished he picked up the telescope and scanned the camp. Eliza Prentice sat between Macomber and the Bailey kid, her hand at her mouth as if she was worried about something. Macomber was shaking his head. Was she asking to be allowed to try walking the ridge by herself? Did she know there was another way in? Cal ran a finger over the raw scar across his scalp, wondering how much she knew, and how much she'd given away to Macomber. She'd been too young to remember that trail leading into the hills, but her father could have told her it was there.

*

A fresh volley of shots rang out, and Cal jolted awake. The sun would soon rise on yet another day. At first sight the dim light of the dawn showed nothing had changed. He lifted his head and a splinter of stone spat past his cheek, while another slug whined overhead, ricocheting off the slab of rock that hung low above his hiding place. Cal ducked back, and the posse wasted a few more bullets before silence fell. By now they'd marked every position he'd used to fire on them over the last two days, and this time it looked like they planned to keep him pinned down.

The light grew. If Cal showed so much as a hair the posse started up a relentless hail of lead. He lay back against the rock in the lookout, his heart pounding. They were going to bust through. He'd got a glimpse of the camp and seen horses saddled and ready. Any time now riders would come galloping up through the gulch and on into the shadows beyond.

Cal raced down from the lookout, trying to find a place they hadn't got covered, but he fired just one shot before the posse had him spotted again. The gunfire was constant, and far too accurate for comfort. He worked up a sweat trying to snap off an occasional shot, but mostly he was driven back into cover before he could seek out a target. When he next caught sight of the camp some of the horses had gone.

In desperation Cal ran to the top of the rocky plateau, then lowered himself down the face of the cliff until he could look over into the narrow gulch. Three riders, Glenn Macomber on his roan in the lead, were making their way up the winding trail. Lying down on a narrow ledge, Cal settled the Henry comfortably against his shoulder, ignoring the crack and whine of bullets hitting the cliff face below him. Holding his breath he squeezed the trigger, but at this range it would be a lucky shot that found its mark, and it looked like his luck was running out. Riding hard and fast, the men forged on without a pause.

Cal had horses ready and waiting. He didn't want to desert the valley, the only place that had felt like home to him since the day he killed Mort Bailey, but there were no choices left to make. With Glenn Macomber's help Eliza Prentice was going to get her wish. He hadn't thought she'd betray him, no matter how much she wanted to come back to her father's land, but he'd been wrong. His lips twisted in a crooked smile, not bitter but sad. Life had dealt Eliza a lousy hand, he couldn't blame her for wanting to take what was hers.

Filled with a sense of loss, Cal glanced at the camp again as he climbed back towards the lookout, hoping to get one last look at Eliza. Another noisy fusillade sent him ducking deeper into cover, but not a single bullet struck the rock face. The shots were no longer being aimed his way. Cal returned to the lookout on all fours, and lifted his head to peer over the stone parapet.

Three riders were charging up the Kentville trail with guns blazing, one of them towing a reluctant pack horse. It looked like reinforcements were coming. Cal recognized Moke Rodway's flashy pinto, and he thought he could hear the man's yelping laughter over the rolling echo of gunfire. The members of the posse who'd been keeping Cal pinned down had been so intent on their job that they'd left their backs exposed, and now they had nowhere to hide from the Hinds gang. One man tried to make a run for it, diving towards a pitifully small pile of rocks in his search for shelter, but a bullet struck him and he fell, to lie face down in the dirt.

Cal knew it was time to leave, but the thought of Eliza held him rooted to the spot. The outlaws rode hell for leather through the camp, flattening her tent and scattering the fire. Then Bart Rodway was in among the posse's remaining horses, the animals squealing as they kicked and reared in terror. He slashed the rope tether with his knife and yelled in triumph as they bolted. Suddenly a slight bareheaded figure was in the midst of the plunging bodies and drumming hoofs, her halo of bright hair unmistakable.

'No!' Cal shouted uselessly, his voice lost in the thunderous noise coming up from the camp as the outlaws and the posse exchanged fire. Moke Rodway changed course, slipping his rifle back into its holster then dragging his horse's head round and aiming straight at the girl. Eliza tried to duck out of the way, but the outlaw leant down and grabbed her by the hair, his other hand taking hold of her arm. With a mighty heave he lifted her across the front of his saddle.

One man had found a place to hide, snugged down in the shallow arroyo. Cal recognized him; it was Seth Bailey. He'd been returning Bart Rodway's fire, but now he came hurtling out of cover to throw himself at Moke, trying to grab the bridle and pull his horse down, but Moke jerked back to take the pinto wheeling away. Dobey Hinds spun his mount and came alongside, bringing the butt of his carbine down hard on Bailey's head. The youngster fell to the ground and didn't stir as the two horses circled over him. Whooping and yelling, firing as they rode, the three riders abandoned the devastation they'd made of the camp and stormed towards the gap that would bring them to the ridge.

CHAPTER TEN

Cal lifted into the saddle. He could escape into the broad grasslands of the valley before the remaining members of the posse came down from the ridge. They might never make it to the cabin; they probably didn't even know the Hinds gang were on their tail. He clapped his spurs to the black's sides and galloped at breakneck speed, back through the gap in the thorn barrier and around the cabin, pulling up outside the barn. Here he hesitated; there was a spare horse ready, his bedroll and supplies were packed. All he had to do was ride away.

But Moke Rodway had Eliza.

Choking off a curse, Cal leapt from the saddle and slapped the black's rump to send it jogging into the barn, pushing the door closed. Eliza had teamed up with Macomber, but he couldn't leave her in the hands of a man like Moke. Even if she felt nothing for him, even if she'd come to see him hunted out of her valley, he'd not turn his back on her now. If just this once luck was on his side he might still get away, and if he did then he'd do his damnedest to take Eliza along. At that moment he didn't care whether she came willing or not.

He hurried to the thorn barrier with the Henry in his

hand, intent on closing the gap. Macomber's men could be here any time. Seth Bailey would have warned the sheriff about the gully that crossed the ridge, and how he'd lost his horse; the kid didn't know about the track that skirted the edge of the cliff, but if the riders didn't find a way to get their horses across they could still come on foot.

Remembering the roughness of the trail along the ridge, Cal reckoned he had time to get into one of the defensive positions the outlaws had set up at the base of the cliff. From either of them he could command the open ground outside the thorn bushes; the posse would never get as far as the cabin. He only had to hold them for a few minutes; Hinds and the Rodway brothers wouldn't be far behind, and they'd close the trap.

He was dragging the barrier across when the man came, running so fast down the slope he was almost losing his footing. Cal spun around. Macomber must have abandoned his horse, probably at the gully, and slid down the mountainside without using the trail. He came to a halt only yards away, grimacing as he gulped in air, his chest heaving.

'Glenn,' Cal said, dropping the rope attached to the barrier, but making no move to draw the Smith & Wesson from its holster. 'I sure wish you hadn't come.'

Macomber said nothing, taking a couple of steps, lifting the rifle he held.

'You never used to be trigger happy, Glenn. You come all this way to shoot me down in cold blood?' Cal stared at the man who had once been his friend.

'Not if you unbuckle that belt and give yourself up,' Macomber said.

From somewhere up the slope a rock came crashing

down the hillside. Macomber jumped, spinning to look for the source of the sound, but whoever had dislodged the rock was still high up the trail. They wouldn't be here for a full minute, maybe more.

But Moke Rodway, riding like the devil himself, was spurring his horse straight down from the ridge, a ride that only a madman would have attempted. He must have seen Macomber's breakneck descent and followed. Eliza still lay across the front of his saddle, her knuckles white as she clung frantically to the man's stirrup.

Moke heaved the plunging pinto to a sliding halt, his long-barrelled Colt lifting to take aim. There was an evil grin on his lips as he fired, so close he couldn't miss.

Macomber had been twisting back towards Cal, and some instinct kept him turning. Instead of taking him full in the back, the slug ploughed a bloody furrow along two ribs, scraping across his backbone before it lodged under a rib on the other side.

The force of the shot spun Macomber around. He fell, slowly, like a tree when the last blow of the axe severs its hold on the ground. The sheriff lay still, the soles of his dusty boots pointing at the sky.

Moke let out a screech of triumph, kneeing the horse around and using the hand that held the rein to clamp down on Eliza who was trying to lift herself off the saddle-bow. He drove his horse at Cal, silver eyes glinting malevolently as he brought the Colt up for another shot.

'No!' Dobey Hinds came riding down the trail with Bart Rodway on his heels and the pack horse sliding sideways between them. Hinds brought his mount alongside Cal, blocking Moke's aim. 'He was holding them off, Moke. That was him firing from the lookout while we were riding in.'

'When I got here him an' the lawman was jawin' real friendly,' Moke protested, 'an' he let you down, you said so. He didn't never mean to come to Silverlode.'

'By the time my business in Kentville was done it was too late,' Cal said.

Moke gave him a baleful look. 'What about him?' he gestured at Macomber's body. 'Lookit you, never even tried to draw.'

'He had the drop on me,' Cal stepped across to pick up the sheriff's rifle. 'I figured I'd keep him talking. It beat taking a bullet.'

'Smart talkin' don't—'

'Shut up Moke,' Hinds cut him off. 'With one posse already here and another on the way, could be we'll want every gun we've got. If this needs talking about we'll do it later.' He turned to Bart. 'You reckon any more of the law's left on the ridge?'

'The big coyote on the bay went over the side, an' his horse with him,' Bart said, twisting in the saddle to try and look at the back of his thigh. 'Think I winged the other one. Wish I'd finished him the bastard plugged me.'

Moke grinned at his brother. 'Reckon they come off worst. That was a mighty interestin' trip home.' He slid the Colt into its holster and finally let the girl wriggle free, landing a less than gentle slap on her buttocks before she dropped to the ground 'An' I found me somethin' that's gonna warm up those winter nights.'

'No,' Cal said, hurrying to help Eliza to her feet, speaking without giving his words a thought. 'She's mine.'

'Whaddya mean, she's yours?' Moke's quicksilver eyes blazed hatred, the pinto moving restlessly beneath him and his hand dropping once more to the butt of his gun.

'While you was hidin' in here sweet-talkin' the sheriff, I took her off that posse. She's mine, fair an' square.'

'I mean,' Cal said, stepping away from Eliza with the sheriff's Winchester cocked, and speaking each word slow and clear, 'that she's my wife.'

Eliza made a sound so faint he doubted if the other men heard it. He half expected her to deny his claim, but instead she ran to fling her arms around him, burying her head against his chest.

'Hard luck, Moke,' Hinds said. 'Guess we know what kept Mason so busy in Kentville.'

'He's lyin'.' Moke was out of the saddle and striding towards them. He spat on the ground at Cal's feet, his disturbing eyes moving restlessly over Eliza's slim frame. 'Come on, girl, tell me he's lyin'.'

Eliza said nothing, merely shaking her head. Cal pushed her aside so she would be out of the line of fire, his finger tightening on the trigger; Moke wasn't the kind to listen to reason.

'Enough! You plan to stand here and argue till the posse arrives?' Hinds spoke with his usual authority. 'We got other troubles.' He looked down at Macomber. 'Looks like you settled with the sheriff, Moke. . . .'

Eliza gasped, her hands going swiftly to her mouth.

'What?' Hinds snapped, turning on her.

'His eyes,' she said, staring at the sheriff. 'He opened his eyes.'

'Hell,' Moke said, cocking the long barrelled revolver, 'if you won't let me deal with Mason at least I can fix that.'

'No. I want him alive.' Cal stepped forward, his fingers fastening on Moke's wrist with a grip like a steel hawser. His other hand reached to take the gun and send it spinning away. 'You leave him be.'

'No interferin', cheatin', lyin' yellowbelly tells me what to do!' Moke's fury boiled up, his voice rising to a shriek. Unable to release himself from Cal's grasp, he kicked out with his foot, his boot smashing into Cal's knee. He'd kept hold of the pinto's rein, and he flipped it wide, spinning it over Cal's head, ready to haul it around his neck, yelling to urge the horse into motion. Cal didn't wait for the rawhide to tighten, ducking away so the rein caught on his arm instead. At the same time he heaved on Moke's wrist with every ounce of his strength.

They fell together, sprawling across Macomber's legs, Moke on top, his free hand slamming at Cal's throat. The pinto's rein tautened as the animal tried to escape, jerking Cal's arm so hard he thought his shoulder might pull out. Cal slammed a knee up and Moke grunted in pain, attempting to push himself clear before another blow landed, but Cal stuck like a burr, not releasing his grip on the younger man's arm. With the pinto's rein still tight round Cal's wrist, the two men rolled under the horse's hoofs. Moke's fingers clawed for Cal's eyes, and Cal thrust his head back just in time, though Moke's fingernails left angry red trails down his cheek.

Squealing in protest, the pinto pranced, eager to escape from this madness, its hoofs seeking for solid ground and finding only yielding flesh as the men pummelled each other beneath its belly. The rein seared a burn across the back of Cal's hand, where it was trapped under Moke's back. Throwing up its head, the pinto pulled back so hard that the rein snapped close to the bit. The horse lashed out in anger as it leapt away, and a steel-shod hoof struck Cal a glancing blow, drawing blood from the freshly healed scar on his scalp.

'Stop this!' The butt of Hinds' gun smote the side of Moke's head, and the younger man yelped in pain. Cal still hadn't released Moke's wrist, and Hinds cracked the gun down on his fingers, forcing him to let go. 'Quit right now, or so help me I'll finish the pair of you.'

The two men broke apart, coming to their feet to stand glaring at each other.

'I already said we don't have time for this,' Dobey Hinds said, his voice dangerously quiet. 'There's still some of the posse unaccounted for. Not to mention there's likely more lawmen riding up from Silverlode who could be here any time. Moke, your brother's hurt. Best get him inside and see what you can do for him. You,' – he nodded coldly at Cal – 'get that pack horse unloaded.'

'Sure,' Cal said, nodding towards Eliza. 'My wife can come and help.'

'No. I don't want you two fighting over her while I'm not around. I'm going up to the lookout, she'd best come too.'

'There's fresh horses in the barn,' Cal offered.

'Fresh horses?' Hinds queried. 'Where'd they come from?'

'Some friends of yours dropped by. They didn't bother to introduce themselves, just started slinging lead.' Cal fingered the scar. 'Seems they didn't like the look of me.'

'They ain't the only ones,' Moke said.

'Enough!' Hinds roared.

Bart rode past the barrier to the barn, where he eased slowly down from his saddle and looked inside. 'I seen that big bay before. Belongs to Hambo.'

'Belonged,' Cal corrected him. 'Sure hope you weren't too attached.'

'Hambo's dead?'

Cal nodded. 'When men start shooting at me I'm inclined to shoot back.'

'You hear that?' Moke spat, turning furiously to Hinds. 'You gonna let that pass?'

'Hambo always was a fool,' Hinds said shortly. 'Guess he took on more'n he could handle.'

'What about him?' Moke asked, jerking his head towards Macomber then turning to face Hinds again. 'I put a bullet in him, and I say he's mine. Ain't no business of Mason's what happens to him.'

Hinds shrugged, looking at Cal. 'Give me one good reason for keeping him alive.'

'I'll give you two. The sheriff was in Kentville before he rode out here. It's likely he knows how many men will be in the posse that's following you, and who's leading it. That kind of information could be useful. And maybe he can tell us when they'll likely get here.'

'That's one,' Hinds assented.

'Ain't nothin',' Moke sneered.

Hinds quelled him with a look. 'What's the second?'

'Not a lawman this side of the mountains hasn't heard of Glenn Macomber. Reckon they'll think twice about riding in here if they know we're holding him. It'll be real handy if we need to trade. A dead man's worth nothing.'

Hinds seemed to consider this for a while then he nodded. 'All right. Get him inside and see what you can do for him. Moke, you leave Mason alone while I'm gone. And the sheriff.'

Cal replaced the pad of cloth he'd used as a bandage and straightened, rubbing a bloody hand over his aching forehead. He hadn't managed to remove the slug from Macomber's back. The sheriff had been unconscious for a while now, but his breathing didn't sound too bad, and when Cal put his fingers against the man's neck he could feel a steady pulse.

Going to the stove, Cal poured himself a coffee. Outside the window the sky was darkening; the day was almost over. He wondered if he should ride up to the look-out and check on Hinds and Eliza.

Moke came out of the little back room followed by his brother. Bart was limping worse than before as he crossed the room, and his face was grey. He shouldered Cal aside and grabbed the coffee pot.

The hours that had passed since the fight hadn't sweetened Moke's temper any, and he was ready to start it again. He eyed Cal across the table.

'Be dark soon, time a man gets kinda lonely,' he said. 'See, I fetched that girl,' he added, 'took her off the posse, all by myself, an' I still say she's mine.' He turned in appeal to his brother, who had taken a whiskey bottle out of his pocket to pour a generous measure into his coffee.

Bart drank thirstily before he replied.

'Fair shares,' he said, lips parting in an evil grin. 'That's how it works. But seein' it's you, little brother, I won't argue about who gets her first.'

'She's not. . . .' Cal began, but then Dobey Hinds came in, with Eliza Prentice trailing behind him. She had a bruise on her cheek that Cal hadn't noticed before. 'What. . . ?'

'I'm all right,' she said hastily.

'Never did like havin' women around,' Hinds grumbled, throwing his hat on the table. 'You'd better find her

some place out of my way, Mason. I don't want to be trip-
ping over her every few minutes.'

'There's room in the feed shed,' Cal said. 'Both of us'll
move out there.' He glanced at Moke, who was fingering
the butt of the Colt. 'I figure her cooking might be worth
a try.'

Hinds nodded. 'Fine. But that's the only time she gets
to come in here.'

'If that's the way you want it.' Cal jerked his head at
Eliza, then headed to the corner where he kept his
bedroll. 'Go ahead, I'll bring out some blankets.'

As the girl passed Moke he grabbed her left hand and
jerked it up so Hinds could see. 'Lookit there,' he said
triumphantly. 'Ain't got no weddin' ring. I knew Mason
was lyin'.'

Cal straightened up and stared at Moke and Eliza,
stone-faced.

Moke was grinning. 'I ain't greedy like you, Mason,' he
said. 'Reckon I'll share her if you ask real pretty.'

'I'm sorry,' Eliza said, ignoring Moke although he was
still grasping her wrist so tight that her fingers were turning white. She spoke directly to Cal as if they were alone in
the room. 'I'm real sorry, Cal, you've got every right to be
angry.' Her free hand fumbled at the neck of her shirt,
and she pulled out a thin chain. Hanging on it was a gold
band. She slipped the ring on her finger; it fitted perfectly.

'I had to take it off; please don't be mad.' Eliza bit her
lip as she looked up at Cal, who was still staring at her in
silence. 'I couldn't let the sheriff know we were married,
could I? He never would have brought me here.'

'Reckon you'd better let her go,' Cal said quietly,
moving his gaze to Moke's restless silver eyes. Moke shot a

fleeting glance at Hinds.

'You got us in enough trouble,' Hinds said, 'you and your women. Leave her be.'

With a curse Moke threw Eliza's hand away from him and flung out of the door.

Eliza came to Cal then, and for the second time that day she was in his arms, her body trembling as she pressed against him. Cal sank his face into the mass of bright hair to hide his confusion. His head was throbbing. Could a man take a wife and not remember? Standing with her yielding softness against his body and the scent of her hair filling his head, he felt like he was drowning.

CHAPTER ELEVEN

'Women have their uses,' Hinds conceded, pushing back from the table. 'It's a while since I ate home cooking.'

'Some of 'em are good at doctorin',' Bart Rodway said, leering at Eliza as she carried away the last of the plates. 'Could make herself real useful.' He fumbled with the buttons of his pants. 'I'm mighty sore, ma'am. Want to give a poor sick man a helpin' hand?'

Eliza flushed, shaking her head at Cal as he scowled and half rose from his stool. Lighting a candle from the lamp that stood by the door she disappeared into the lean-to at the side of the cabin which served as a scullery, and there were loud noises of tin plates being thrown into a bucket, then the slam of the outer door.

Bart laughed, then shifted awkwardly on his seat, wincing. 'See here, Dobey, if I'm ever gonna sit a horse again, somebody better get this lead out of my butt. Moke come close to takin' my leg off but he didn't dig out that damn slug.'

'Hell, Bart, I did my best,' Moke protested. 'You wouldn't keep still.'

'How could I, with you twistin' that blade so hard it felt like you was tryin' to fillet me?'

'It can't be that hard,' Hinds said. He looked at the motionless form of Glenn Macomber, lying in a corner on Cal's bedroll. 'How about it, Mason, are you a better doctor than Moke?'

'No,' Cal replied. 'Bullet's still in him, too. It's in deep, stuck under the bone.'

'Maybe you need a longer knife,' Bart suggested, pulling a hunting knife from a sheath on his belt. 'One time I stuck this under a man's ribs and it come clear out of his back. Though he was just a little runt of a half-breed.'

'I don't know enough about what's in a man's insides to go poking around,' Cal replied evenly. 'Figured I'd do more harm than good if I kept trying.'

'Moke said the sheriff was conscious for a while,' Hinds said. 'Did you ask him about that posse?'

'I asked,' Cal nodded. 'He told me the men from Silverlode will likely be here tomorrow. Posse's led by a federal marshal by the name of Gallagher. Macomber said he never met him, but he's supposed to be a good lawman.'

'There's no such thing, not till they're dead,' Moke said, grinning savagely, 'though I figure Macomber's gonna be real good, anytime now. You shoulda let me finish him. Hell, you'd put down a horse with a busted leg, so why leave a damn lawman sufferin'? If this Gallagher don't know him, ain't no reason why he'd trade for Macomber's life.'

Cal glanced towards the scullery. 'You think that's why I didn't want him to die quick and easy?' he said quietly, leaning over the table so his face was only inches away from Moke's. 'Thanks to Macomber I've been six months on the run. Six months with nothing to eat but rotten meat and stale biscuit, and riding so hard I got saddle sores on my saddle sores. He owes me, and I'll see he pays. In full.'

There was a disturbing brightness in Moke's eyes as he returned Cal's gaze. 'Now *that* makes sense,' he said. 'Why didn't you say so in the first place?'

'With Eliza listening? Womenfolk don't like to hear things like that.' Cal shrugged. 'Seems Macomber treated her like a lady.'

Moke laughed. 'Man's a fool then, ain't he? Just like you.'

The outer door opened and closed, and the sound of water being poured came from the scullery.

'Don't do to spoil women,' Moke went on, raising his voice a little. 'They're like horses, need to know who's boss. You wanna get yourself a quirt an' some real sharp spurs.' He glanced at Macomber, still unmoving in his corner, apparently unconscious. 'Anytime you need any help handlin' him, Mason, you only gotta ask old Moke. I spent a few weeks holed up with an Apache one time, learnt me a whole lot. Hell, them redskins know things I never even thought of.'

'I don't need that kind of help,' Cal said. 'He won't last long if I can't get that bullet out, maybe won't live through the night if he's treated rough.' He stared at Moke, his eyes hard. 'And I don't want him dying on me.'

'Never mind the damn sheriff, what about me?' Bart broke in. 'I wanna ride out of here one day, an' I don't plan to sit side-saddle.'

'There's a man with the posse who knows how to deal with bullet wounds,' Eliza had come back quietly into the room, carrying a coffee pot. She kept her gaze firmly fixed on the table as the men looked at her.

'You sayin' they got a doc ridin' with 'em?' Bart asked, holding up his mug for her to fill.

'Not a doctor, but a man who spent nearly two years back East, learning how to be one.' She looked across at Cal. 'It's Seth Bailey, you know. He was studying medicine, but when his father died he couldn't afford to carry on. It seems that since he came out West that's about the first thing he was asked to do, take a slug out of a man's arm. He was hoping his uncle would pay for him to stay on at the hospital, but he wanted him to work on the Bar Zee instead. Seth went to the ranch thinking he might change his mind.'

'Only by the time he got there, Mort Bailey was dead.' Every one of them spun around at the sound of Glenn Macomber's voice. He stared up at them, eyes fever bright as he ground out the words between gritted teeth, the effort obviously paining him. 'Cal Mason killed him.'

'Maybe it would be easier in the morning, when there's more light,' Eliza said, flickering shadows playing around the rough wooden walls of the feed shed as she lifted the lamp a little higher. Outside the daylight had gone from the valley where the cabin lay, although the sky above was still bright.

'No, it was light enough when I tried before,' Cal replied, laying down his knife and putting the blood-stained cloth back over the messy gouge in Macomber's back. 'And don't let his strong-man act fool you – I doubt he'll last long if we can't do something about that bullet. There's bits of his vest stuck in the wound; they'll turn it bad. I've seen that happen before.'

'Can't we get him back to the camp somehow? I'm sure Seth could help him.'

'You think Hinds and the Rodways would let me do that?' Cal shook his head. 'The only reason Glenn's still alive is because Moke thinks I've got plans to make him suffer.'

'I wondered about that. Why are you trying to help him?' Eliza asked, as she hung the lamp up beside the door. 'He was the one who put a price on your head. And you said yourself, he's been chasing you for months.'

Cal rinsed the blood off his hands and dried them on a piece of burlap, then he turned to her, his face sombre. 'He's a good man. And we were friends once. I can't stand by and watch him die, no matter what he thinks of me.'

'He thinks you're a murderer,' Eliza said, staring up at Cal, her blue eyes looking very large in the dim light. 'But I don't believe it. You're a decent man. A murderer wouldn't have put his own life on the line to save him from Moke that way.' She came closer and gently touched the scar on his forehead. 'Maybe you're not a murderer. Could be it's a mistake. Your memory's all confused after that bullet hit you.'

Cal shook his head. 'Some things are clear enough. I killed Mort. And as I watched him die I was sure I'd done the right thing.' He sighed. 'What I don't remember is why.'

'What sort of man was Mort Bailey?' She asked.

'That's not an easy question to answer.' Cal gently laid a blanket over Macomber, grateful that the sheriff had sunk back into unconsciousness. 'He was a rancher, richest man in Bannack County, though he started out thirty years ago with nothing. Folks say he worked hard to get what he wanted. Maybe didn't always stick to the law in the early days, but then that was true of a lot of men, including my father. Our spread was across the river from the Bar Zee. We were never exactly friendly, but Bailey played fair when it came to roundup time, and after I took over the ranch we drove our cattle to the railhead together a couple times.'

'Were he and the sheriff good friends?'

'Not special. Not like me and Glenn. Trouble is, Glenn Macomber is a lawman first, a friend second. I guess that's how he sees it. I broke the law when I killed Mort. Whatever reason I had for doing it, it wasn't enough to stop Glenn putting a price on my head and tracking me here. Don't reckon I'll be able to talk my way out of a murder charge.'

'Not even if you save his life?'

'Don't seem likely.' He rubbed the scar again. 'You're right, that darned slug sure messed up my memory. There's this idea keeps bothering me. Seth Bailey wasn't even around when I shot his uncle, but I've got this feeling he knows something, something real important.'

Eliza's eyes lit up. 'Maybe we could take the sheriff back to camp and ask Seth about it at the same time.'

Cal picked up her hand in his own. 'Don't want much, do you? Sure, we could maybe sneak out at night, but I'd bet Hinds will be keeping a close eye on the horses. If we got lucky we might get across the ridge, but I'm not about to walk all the way to Canada.'

Her forehead creased as she thought this over. 'Couldn't we come back? And tell them the sheriff had escaped?'

'They'd never believe it. Besides, I reckon carrying him that far would kill him,' Cal said. 'Might kill me too,' he added, a small smile lifting the corners of his mouth. 'He's no light weight.'

'Then we'll have to get Seth to come here.'

'Just go and ask him?' Cal's smile broadened. 'You sure do have some dandy ideas.'

'We could tell Hinds we were bringing help for Bart.'

Cal shook his head. 'Even if Hinds fell for that, I doubt if Bailey would come. What's in it for him? He's not going to walk unarmed into an outlaw's hideout, to take a bullet out of a murderer and another out of a lawman he hardly knows.'

'I don't know. It's the sort of thing a good doctor would be willing to do, and Seth was real mad about not being able to finish his schooling.' She tightened her grip on Cal's arm when he looked doubtful. 'There has to be a way. If Seth doesn't want to come then we'll make him. We could go in the middle of the night. There aren't many men camped out there now, three or four, that's all. And one of them twisted his ankle trying to climb to the ridge in the dark, he can hardly hobble.'

When Cal didn't respond, Eliza let go of him and turned away, her shoulders sagging. 'I know, I'm being silly. If only there was some way of getting out of the valley without anybody knowing.'

'There is,' Cal said, staring down at Macomber, his brows knitted into a frown. 'The trail your father made, to get his cattle and supplies in here. I found it a while ago.'

'Then we can do it!' she looked triumphant.

'Maybe. I guess it's the only chance he's got.' He was silent again, thinking hard. If he made the attempt while he was on guard, he might be able to leave without Hinds or the Rodways knowing. It was a long ride up the valley and down through the hidden canyon though, and he wouldn't have much time to spare. Then there'd be Bailey to deal with; if the man made so much as a squeak while they were close to the camp, he could end up dead.

'One thing's sure,' Cal said at last. 'If I'm going to do it, then it has to be tonight. There's that posse from Silverlode on the way.' Another problem hit him. He looked at Eliza, who was standing watching him with a trusting expression on her face. 'I don't like leaving you here alone.'

'I can bar the door,' she said.

Cal shook his head doubtfully. She'd probably be safe enough for a few hours, but if anything happened to him she'd be trapped in the valley. With Moke.

A quarter-moon was climbing into the sky. A shadow moved across in front of the distant camp-fire, a man bending to lift the coffee pot off the glowing embers.

'They've set a guard.' Eliza shivered, though it wasn't cold; the rocks at their back were still warm from the heat of the sun. 'Maybe you shouldn't go.'

'I have to. Once I've given Dobey time to hit the sack.' Cal had half expected trouble when he brought the girl to share his watch, figuring she'd be safer away from Moke, but Dobey Hinds had made no protest, maybe because they'd ridden double to the lookout on Cal's black; there was no way they could run out on the gang with only one horse between the two of them.

Her hand felt for his and he grasped her fingers, surprised at how cold they were. 'I'd best leave you my coat,' he said, easing out of it and draping it over her shoulders. 'You know what to do if the posse makes a move?'

'I'll fire the shotgun into the air,' she said.

'Aiming it that way,' Cal reminded her, 'so they'll hear it in the cabin.'

'You're the one who lost his memory, not me,' she said, a smile in her voice. She took his head between her hands, pulling it down until she could press her lips against the scar. 'You didn't forget me, did you? When this happened?'

'Forget you?' He grinned into the darkness. 'I couldn't get you out of my head. If you knew some of the dreams I had! Compared to me you'd think Moke was a gentleman and Sears was a saint.'

'It's all right for a married man to think that way about his wife,' she replied, 'even if we haven't quite got round to making our vows yet.'

'And that's another thing,' Cal said. 'For a while there I wondered if we'd made it to church and I'd forgotten about it! Where did you get that gold band? I've been going over and over what I can remember about those days I spent with you in Kentville, but I don't recall we bought a ring.'

'It was my mother's, the only thing of hers I managed to keep hidden from Amelia Sears. As soon as I realized the sort of people they really were I buried it in their back yard.' She laughed. 'I wasn't brave enough to go and dig it up again, so after you'd left I paid a little boy to do it. He had his friends make a noise outside the front of the house to keep Sears busy. Of all the money you got for me, that was the best fifty cents I spent.'

Her fingers moved a little in his. 'When I said we were married, when Moke wanted to fight you, I wasn't sure what you were going to do. You looked as if you'd been pole-axed. I didn't mean to do that to you, but he. . . .'

'If he lays his filthy hands on you one more time I'll kill him,' Cal said evenly. 'Guess that's what I was thinking at the time. Though it sure was a shock. I'd spent days trying to work out what was real, and in the end I figured no woman was going to tie herself to a man like me. I decided those things we said to each other in Kentville were just a dream.'

'If they were then it's a dream I had too. And we'll make it come true,' she promised. 'I'm yours and you're mine, and nobody's going to change that.'

CHAPTER TWELVE

There was a faint sound as Cal's boot touched a loose stone, and he froze. He was only yards from the camp-fire, burnt down now to a red glow, but still bright enough to blind his eyes to the comparative darkness surrounding it. There had to be a guard, though he didn't have him spotted yet. It had taken Cal time to work around so he'd approach downwind; if the horses had caught his scent they might have given the alarm. The short summer night was passing and he needed to hurry.

Before he could get the drop on Seth Bailey he had to silence the man who was on watch. A few moments ago he'd seen movement over by the horse-line, and he didn't think it was one of the animals. Slow and silent, he eased down to hands and knees, then to his belly. Holding one hand between his eyes and the fire to improve his night sight, he waited until the shapes of horses could be guessed at. One of them was a paler colour than the rest; Macomber had been riding a roan, perhaps the animal had made it back off the ridge without its rider.

Cal breathed a silent sigh of relief. He'd found the guard. The man was standing with his back to the horses, head slightly bent as he looked towards the fire, apparently lost in thought. He was tall, and bulky. Cal tried to recall what he'd seen of the posse; only two of them were that kind of size. It was just possible he'd located Seth Bailey.

Squirming along in the dirt a few inches at a time, working his way ever closer, Cal tried to figure out his next move. He'd left the black in a fold of land not far from the old trail that led down from the valley; horses were sociable animals, always ready to announce the arrival of another of their kind. It meant a long walk with his captive, if he was successful. He had to keep Bailey silent, but knocking him out cold wasn't a good idea, since he couldn't carry the man that far. Cal drew in a long shallow breath as a horse changed its weight from one hind leg to the other, swishing its tail; the nearer he got the more likely it was the animals would get restive.

The other three remaining members of the posse were lying bundled up around the fire. Cal froze as one of them shifted a little. Bart claimed to have winged a man during the fight on the ridge; the pain from the wound might keep him wakeful. A low voice mumbled something, but the man's words made no sense; he was maybe feverish and talking in his sleep. The bedroll rustled as the man turned over.

For a long moment Cal waited, but there was no more movement, and soon a soft rhythmic snore came from under the blanket. Over by the horse-line, the guard hadn't moved either, and Cal resumed his slow approach. The man had made himself comfortable, propping a hip on the long-dead remnant of a tree, his shoulders slouched and his head down. Beside him a shotgun rested against the same dead wood, butt down, the end of the barrel a couple of inches away from the man's left hand.

A half-burnt twig spluttered as it fell into the heart of the embers and there was a brief burst of flame. Cal grinned to himself as he inched forward again. Luck was on his side; in the flicker of light he'd got a good look at the sentry's face. It was Seth Bailey. The man was away from the rest of the posse, and he was sound asleep.

On second thoughts a sleeping man in a bedroll would have been easier to handle. If Bailey yelled . . . Cal felt a touch of fear, cold down his back. Not for himself, but for Eliza. He couldn't bear to think what would happen to her if he failed. If he didn't make it back to the valley there'd be nobody to protect her from Moke. He hesitated, though only for a second. Silently he slid his knife from its sheath.

Still flat on the ground, Cal crooned a few soft notes, wordless sounds aimed at the horses' keen senses, too quiet to reach the sleepers by the fire. A long head with a crooked white blaze turned towards him as he lifted to his knees. Cal's heart lurched, but the animal merely huffed down its nose, unconcerned by his approach. The roan pricked its ears lazily at him, then let them drop out sideways again, recognizing him as human but losing interest when it caught no scent of food.

It was almost too easy. Positioning himself so he could keep an eye on the sleepers by the camp-fire, Cal stepped behind Seth Bailey. He took a deep breath to steady his pounding heart, then very gently he took hold of the rifle and laid it on the ground behind him. Standing again, he laid the flat of the knife's blade across Bailey's throat, his other hand taking a grip of the youngster's wrist to jerk the arm high behind his back. 'One wrong move, just so much as a squeak,' Cal breathed, 'and you're a dead man.'

Cal cursed long and loud. Beside him Seth Bailey sprawled in the dirt yet again.

'Get up.' Cal had lost count of the times he'd helped the youngster back to his feet. He'd already loosened the ropes that tied Bailey's hands in front of him, but they were still going at a snail's pace.

Bailey was silent, just as he'd been ever since he'd woken with Cal's knife at his throat. Once they were away from the camp Cal had removed the bandanna he'd used as a gag, but Bailey showed no inclination to talk.

'What the hell were you doing riding with that posse?' Cal demanded, prodding Bailey into motion again. 'You ain't fit to be walking to the Sunday social.' The night was passing, and his curses were as much for himself as for Bailey. He should have taken a horse. Broken bones mended, but it took time for a man to get his strength back, and Bailey hadn't had that time.

His prisoner didn't answer, merely limping on doggedly and Cal fell into step behind. Then he halted, struck by something else he hadn't thought through. Dammit, he'd got nothing right.

'Hold it,' he ordered. 'You're halfway to being a doctor, ain't that so?'

Bailey half turned, the moonlight shining full upon his face. It was the first time Cal had seen his captive properly, and what he saw brought him to an abrupt halt. Bailey had been surprised by the question, but what struck Cal was the expression of sheer terror on the younger man's face.

'Well?' Cal prompted, when Bailey still didn't break his silence.

The other man nodded slowly.

'Then I guess you've got tools, medicines, a bag maybe.'

'I'm not a doctor yet,' Bailey said, finding his voice at last, his tone wary, as if he suspected some kind of trap. 'But I carry a few things around. I hung onto them when Uncle Mort invited me to work at the ranch, just in case. And the sheriff said to bring them along when I took charge of that first posse that came after you.' His lips twisted in a humourless grin. 'Only one who got hurt that time was me, it wasn't easy setting my own leg.'

'Where are they, these things?'

Bailey jerked his head. 'Wrapped up with my bedroll, back there.'

'Jeez!' Cal groaned. 'Sit down. Stretch your legs out. I'll have to leave you here a while.' There was silence as he tied Bailey's ankles together.

'You . . .' Bailey half choked on the word, and Cal could almost smell his fear. 'That's what this is about . . . somebody's hurt?'

'You think I came looking for you because I was hankering after your company?' Cal pulled the last knot tight. 'Not that I'd object to kicking somebody's butt,' he added, with a grin. 'Fact is, we got two gunshot wounds for you to tend. Glenn Macomber's hurt pretty bad.'

'I . . .' Bailey swallowed noisily. 'I don't have a proper bag. My instruments are in a rolled up package, wrapped in oilskin. You'll find it beside my saddle-bags.'

Cal nodded. 'Fine. Reckon I saw your bedroll alongside the others. Don't you go trying anything while I'm gone,' he said, giving the youngster a tap on the shoulder to emphasize his warning, surprised to feel him flinch. He couldn't figure what Bailey was so scared of; even when the

110

kid lay trapped and helpless under his dead horse he'd been defiant, he'd shown no fear of Cal even when his life hung in the balance. Cal gave a mental shrug as he ran back towards the camp; there was no time to puzzle over it now, he had to hustle. And he'd better hope none of the posse had woken up in the meantime.

The sky was growing paler by the minute. Cal eased the sweating black to a walk, letting go his hold on Bailey as the pace slowed; it must have been an uncomfortable ride for the kid, lying head down across the saddle. Once he'd returned with Bailey's doctoring gear, Cal had decided it was quicker to fetch his horse than try dragging the youngster any further on foot, with his lame leg. With light already showing in the east, he'd been in too much of a hurry to stop and untie his prisoner, just tossing him onto the black and spurring up into the hills.

Before them the cabin was a darker shadow under its protective cliffs, but already Cal could make out the shape of it, along with the larger bulk of the ramshackle outbuildings. He stiffened suddenly. A man, walking slow and furtive, was heading past the barn.

Ignoring Bailey's grunt of protest, Cal spurred the weary horse to a gallop. The man outside the feed shed spun around at the sound of hoofs, his hand going to the holster at his hip.

'Morning, Moke,' Cal shouted. 'Looking for something?'

'What the hell?' Moke Rodway stared, as Cal brought the black to a sliding halt. With a quick heave he dropped Bailey off the saddle so he landed awkwardly at the outlaw's feet.

'Brought your brother a present,' Cal said, lifting down from the horse's back, and reaching to take Bailey's bundle out from inside his vest. 'Nearest thing to a doctor he's likely to get out here. Even brought something better than that knife of yours to cut the bullet out.'

'You were supposed to be on watch,' Moke said, scowling. 'That posse might've—'

'If that posse had looked like moving on us you'd have been warned,' Cal interrupted him. 'and if it's my wife you're looking for, she's not home right now.'

The sound of voices brought Dobey Hinds out of the cabin, followed by Bart Rodway, who limped as far as the hitching rail and stood leaning on it, pale-faced and sweating.

'Ugly one with the sore leg's your patient,' Cal told Bailey, untying his ankles and wrists.

'You ain't got no business ridin' out at night,' Moke growled. 'An' how come you was up there?' He jerked his head at the valley, the way Cal had come.

'Found an easier way off the ridge, stayed on it a little longer before I headed down.' Cal turned to Hinds. 'Could be a problem if the posse ever get through; they could maybe come in back of us.' He didn't think Bailey would have seen much on his wild ride, though the youngster must know he was lying, that they hadn't come over the ridge. With luck he'd know better than to mention it. Cal thrust the oilskin package into Bailey's hands. 'Here, you'll be needing these.'

Hinds followed Cal as he led the black into the barn, watching through narrowed eyes as he unsaddled. 'You were supposed to be keeping watch.'

'Me and Eliza,' Cal reminded him. 'She's still up there.

112

Left her the shotgun in case the posse moved. Figure I'll take me a fresh horse and fetch her, this one's tuckered out. You sending Moke up to take his turn in the lookout?'

Hinds didn't answer. 'It looks like you rode that horse hard,' he commented. 'You sure you found another way off the ridge?'

Cal grinned. 'How else do you figure I got here? Horse is good, but it can't jump over mountains. You want me to show you?' He carried his saddle to the horse that had once belonged to Titch Wilkie. 'I guess Eliza can wait a while.'

'Later.' Hinds turned away. 'Stay at the lookout till one of us comes. And this time do as you're told.'

Cal watched him go, then he led the fresh horse out of the barn, hoping Bailey had the sense to keep his mouth shut. He wished he'd made a point of it, maybe threatened him, but it was too late for regrets. Cal lifted wearily into the saddle; it had been another long night. He wondered why Seth Bailey had been so scared; as soon as he recognized Cal's voice back at the camp the youngster had come along as meek as a lamb. Still pondering the kid's strange behaviour, Cal rode through the growing light up to the lookout.

'I couldn't see you!' Eliza ran down the steep slope, loose rock sliding under her boots. She threw herself into his arms and clung to him. 'I was so afraid. I spent the whole night staring through that fool telescope, but I couldn't see. . . .' There were tears pouring down her face.

'I'm here. It's all right.' Gently Cal wiped the wetness from her cheeks. 'Don't reckon any woman's cried over me since my ma died.' He stroked her hair, cool and damp under his fingers. 'Are you cold?' he asked, feeling her body shiver.

'Not now. But a while ago . . . There was a lot of noise, they were shouting. I thought maybe you were still there, that they'd found you.'

He grinned. 'More likely they were rounding up their horses.'

'You did it? You really brought him back?' She noticed the horse then, recognizing it as one that had been in the barn when they'd left the cabin the night before. 'That's . . . what happened?'

'The sun came up.' He took her arm and led her back up the rocky track. 'Long story.' He yawned. 'Seeing we've got to stay here for a while I guess telling you about it will help me stay awake. Hinds will probably send Moke up, soon as he's had some breakfast, unless he comes himself.'

They stood as they had in the darkness a few hours before, arms around each other, staring at the camp down below. It was full daylight now, the sun already making a shimmer of haze over the distant prairie. Cal's eyes strayed to the far horizon and he straightened suddenly. 'You got the telescope?'

A group of riders were coming, a long string of them, riding hard and fast. 'Oh Jeez. That posse's making pretty good time.' Cal sighed, his body aching for a rest he knew he wasn't going to get. 'Looks like we're heading for another busy day.'

CHAPTER THIRTEEN

'Is that really the posse?' Eliza's voice shook. 'The sheriff didn't say there'd be so many of them.'

'Maybe Glenn hadn't heard they were bringing an army, or maybe he didn't tell us because he didn't want Hinds to run.' Cal frowned as he stared at the advancing riders through the telescope, trying to bring them into focus. 'Only a fool would chance being caught out in the open with that many men on his tail. Hinds needs to know about this. Not that there's much he can do except sit tight.'

'Shall I fetch the shotgun?' Eliza asked. 'You said they'd come running if they heard it.'

'Be enough shooting before we're done, I reckon,' Cal replied, 'I'd rather not start slinging lead before I have to. With luck Gallagher's going to stop and catch up with what's left of Macomber's men.'

'You really think the four of you can hold off all those men?'

'I don't know, but we don't have much choice but to try. And that means getting the others up here.' Cal started back down towards the horse then stopped. 'Best if I stay, just in case they ride straight in.' He came back to her, taking hold of her hands. Feeling her fingers cold and shaking he closed his own around them.

'Ride back to the cabin,' he said, 'but don't get off the horse. Shout for Hinds, and wait for him to come out. I don't want you anywhere near Moke. If he tries anything. . . .'

'I'll stay out of his way.' She made an attempt at a smile. 'I had to look after myself the last few years, since my mother died. I managed. You have to stop worrying about me.'

Cal shook his head, impatient with her. 'I told you before, Moke's not like Sears. Listen, tell Hinds there's eighteen men at least, maybe twenty. We'll need more guns up here if we're going to keep them off the ridge, if Gallagher tries to come straight in I doubt I'll be able to stop him.'

She nodded and went running down the rough slope. Cal watched her ride away then turned the telescope on the riders again. They came streaming across the prairie towards the little encampment. He tried to count them, but the galloping hoofs were sending up clouds of dust. It looked like a cavalry charge, and he twisted his mouth, knowing the federal marshal in charge was putting on the show for his benefit. 'Five to one, maybe,' he muttered. 'But we got the high ground and we got plenty of cover. They won't take us easy.' There was no reason to suspect they knew there was another way in.

Giving up the attempt to count heads Cal turned his attention back to the camp, and the little group waiting to greet the newcomers. He grinned as he looked at the three men standing by the fire watching the approaching riders, wondering what they'd thought when they discovered Bailey had gone. Creeping back into the camp for Bailey's bundle of medical equipment he'd left by way of the horse line, untying each animal though leaving the reins still looped over the rope. He hadn't run the horses off, not wanting to wake the sleeping lawmen, but when he'd looked back a minute later one horse was already wandering away.

Evidently the animals hadn't gone far; they were already back where they belonged. As for the men, the bandy-legged deputy had his arm in a sling, presumably he'd been the one who'd traded shots with Bart up on the ridge. Once they'd chased down the horses and found none of them missing, likely they'd guess what had happened to Bailey, which meant they knew one of the outlaws was in need of doctoring. They wouldn't know that Macomber was hurt too, probably figuring he was dead. Cal's face hardened; as far as the posse was concerned that would make just one more debt they'd be eager to collect on if they ever caught up with him.

Cal had his rifle loaded and ready, with more ammunition in his pocket and the shotgun propped against the rock by his side. He snugged down out of sight, tucking the Henry into his shoulder. If the newcomers tried a massed attack he'd do his best to hold them until Hinds and the Rodways arrived.

'Reckon they're yeller.' Moke spat, aiming for the steep tumble of rocks below the lookout. 'Hell, we bin here hours, an' all they do is sit on their butts havin' a damn powwow.'

'You in a hurry to die?' Cal asked. He stared at the crowded camp; easy enough to count heads now. 'There's twenty-four men down there after your blood. That's quite some posse. Reckon you boys must have had yourselves a good time in Silverlode.'

'Hell, we didn't want to cause no trouble, just rode in nice an' quiet an' held up the bank, real friendly like. We took things easy, didn't harm nobody. Ruckus started when a damnfool cowboy tried to be a hero outside on the street an' got hisself shot.' Moke smirked and spat again. 'We rode out o' there like smoke, changed hosses just the way Dobey planned. There was a handful of men on our tail but we lost 'em before sunset.'

'Something sure made them mad,' Cal said, 'I never saw that many men in one posse.'

'Reckon that's maybe because we had ourselves a bit of fun the next day. There was this ranch house, place we'd ridden past on our way into town. Me an' Bart figured we'd go an' pay a visit.'

'Just the two of you?'

'Yeah. Dobey had some unfinished business to take care of, so we had twenty-four hours before we was due to meet him at Lowe's Rock. We reckoned we'd be neighbourly an' stop by, seeing there was a pretty little woman been left there all alone. It ain't right the way men go ridin' off and leave their womenfolk. That little lady, she'd only been wearin' a weddin' ring for a couple of months, an' her man left her with just an old man an' a black woman for company.'

There was a look in Moke's eyes that made him look more animal than human. 'Me an' Bart figured it would have been downright unfeelin' if we'd just ridden on by. We done the old man a favour, puttin' him out of his misery real quick, then we had ourselves a party. That woman, why, we soon had her halter broke.'

Keeping a tight hold on his anger, Cal said nothing, his fist tightening its grip on the butt of the Henry.

Moke grinned at him, exploring the gap between his front teeth with a dirty fingernail. 'Wished we coulda stayed longer, we had a damn good time, her an' me an' Bart. It's like I told you, it ain't no good bein' soft with women. An' then there was that little black girl. I ain't never had no appetite for dark skin before, but she was real cute, an' almost as sassy as that wife of yours. See, women like that need handlin' right. When we'd done she was all milk an' honey, an' damn near as temptin' as the white woman.'

Still Cal kept his peace; it was no time to start a fight, not between themselves. But at that moment he was sure of just one thing: he might be an outlaw, a murderer, condemned to be hunted down like Dobey Hinds and the Rodway brothers, but whatever happened in the next few hours, he didn't want to die alongside this man.

Looking towards the hollow where the horses were tethered Cal saw Eliza sitting there in the shade, her head lolling back against the rock face as if she was asleep. She jolted awake suddenly, staring down the trail. A moment later Cal could hear the drumming hoofbeats that had alerted her, and Bart Rodway came into sight. He waved a hand at his brother, climbed stiffly out of the saddle and limped up to them.

'Sure am grateful to you, Mason,' Bart said, leaning over the stone parapet to stare down at the posse. 'That fella you brought fixed me up just fine. Hurts some, but he swore I'd be good as new in a couple weeks.'

'Is he taking a look at Macomber?' Cal asked.

'Well,' Bart drawled, 'guess he could look, if'n he wanted, but that ain't gonna be doin' the sheriff much good.'

'Why?' Cal rounded on him. 'What have you done? Are you saying Macomber's—'

'Nothin' wrong with Macomber, unless you count that slug in his back.' Bait sniggered, looking suddenly a lot like his brother. 'I left our doc trussed up like a steer ready for brandin'. Sure did get him riled. Well, couldn't leave him loose, could I? Not all by hisseif. He'd be on one of them horses an' out o' there.'

'Where's Hinds?' Cal asked.

'Ain't he around someplace?' Bart was surprised. 'Last I saw he was puttin' some stuff in a couple of saddle-bags, straight after he sent Moke up here. Reckoned he was bringin' you boys some more ammunition.'

There was a brief silence. 'You don't figure he'd run out on us?' Moke asked, straightening suddenly.

'Dobey?' Bart shook his head. 'He wouldn't do that. We bin together too long.'

'I don't know, he was kinda riled about our little trip to that ranch. Maybe he figures it's our fault we got half an army on our trail.' Moke looked mistrustfully at Cal. 'Suppose Dobey was right, an' Mason here found some other way of gettin' out? Maybe he's gone lookin' for the trail.'

'No, it don't figure. He didn't pack no food or water in them saddle-bags, he was messin' with them supplies we stole from the minin' office up north, that time we hit the eastbound train.'

Moke thought about this for a moment then grinned. 'Is that so? Reckon I know what he's got planned. I thought he

120

was a damn fool weighing his horse down that way, seein' we was on the run, but he knew what he was doin'. Right now he'll be fixin' up a surprise for them lawmen.'

'What sort of surprise?' Cal asked.

'Can't tell right now, not for sure.' Moke nodded. 'It'll be good though. Old Dobey, he's always comin' up with somethin' new, that's what I like about ridin' alongside a man with brains. He thinks things out, not like me an' Bart. I'll bet that posse's got somethin' comin' they'll never forget.'

'I'm going back to the cabin,' Cal said suddenly, tilting the Henry onto his shoulder. 'The sooner Bailey gets that slug out of Macomber the better.'

'We're gonna need you here,' Moke protested. 'Let the sheriff die. Ain't as if he'll go easy. Reckon he'll make a slow job of it, if'n you don't interfere.'

'You can't go,' Bart agreed. 'That posse could make a move any time. Don't reckon Dobey'll be too happy if you ain't here when they start slingin' lead.'

'If I hear shooting I'll ride right back,' Cal said. 'And I'll make sure Bailey stays put. There's no weapons left in the cabin so he can't do us any harm. It's not as if he can ride out over the ridge; he'd be right in our line of fire.' He didn't think Bailey would try to find his way out through the valley, he'd not seen much of the route the night before.

'You gonna leave the little lady to keep us company?' Moke shouted after him, as Cal hurried down to the horses. His cackling laughter followed them as Cal and Eliza rode away.

'Why?' Glenn Macomber forced the word out through gritted teeth, his face a mask of agony, his hands gripping tight at the edge of the table while Seth Bailey probed at the wound in his back.

'Why what?' Cal asked, leaning down hard on the man's shoulders so he couldn't move, knowing that Macomber was trying to keep his mind off the pain. Remembering what he'd gone through when Hambo's bullet grazed his skull, Cal could understand. 'Hold on, Glenn, he's almost got it. Keep talking, if it helps any.'

With sweat pouring from him, the words coming out jerkily between rasping gasps for breath, the sheriff turned his head a little more, his eyes resting on Eliza who stood holding a bowl of water, her face set and white. 'She shouldn't be here,' he said.

'Her choice,' Cal said shortly. 'Come on, Glenn, that wasn't what you were talking about. Why what?'

'Why did you fetch Seth out here? Why are you so set on keeping me alive?'

It wasn't the question he'd expected. Cal was silent a moment, thinking about it. What he'd told Eliza had a certain truth to it – he and the sheriff had been good friends. He hadn't wanted him to die. But there was something else, something that maybe Macomber knew. Or maybe he didn't.

Cal looked up and his eyes met those of Seth Bailey. Again he could see the haunted look in them. More than fear, it was sheer terror. Macomber gave an involuntary grunt of pain as Bailey's hand jerked. The younger man stepped back, rubbing the back of his hand over his forehead, looking down, unwilling to risk meeting Cal's gaze again.

'I figured,' Cal said slowly, 'that maybe you could tell me something about Mort. About the reason why he died.'

'Me? You crazy?' Macomber's face cracked into a travesty of a smile. 'You trying to tell me you weren't there? Hell, Cal, I ain't that much of a fool.'

'No, I don't reckon you are.' Cal kept his eyes on Bailey. 'This maybe isn't the time to talk about this. Go on, doc, get that damn slug out. And make sure you do a good job, I've seen what happens when there's bits of cloth and stuff stuck in a bullet wound.'

'Yeah, come on, Seth,' Macomber agreed. 'Get it done. Feels like I got a wildcat gnawing at my back.'

Bailey drew in a deep breath and returned to work, pulling back again, but this time with a bloody misshapen lump of metal clasped between the jaws of the forceps in his hand. It took a few more minutes to clean the mangled flesh, then he nodded to Eliza to bind the wound. 'If it doesn't turn bad you'll be on your feet in a few days,' he said.

Macomber grunted. 'Thanks. It feels just dandy.'

'Sure it does,' Cal said, releasing his grip on the sheriff's shoulders. He straightened, looking across at Bailey. 'Seeing you're finished with Glenn it's time you talked to me.'

'I don't . . . I didn't . . .' Bailey took an involuntary step backwards. 'He didn't tell me anything, I swear. . . .'

'Who didn't?' Cal followed him, his hands clenching into fists. 'What. . . .' From the distance came a rattle of gunfire, a dozen shots or more.

'Seems like this has to wait.' Reluctantly Cal abandoned Bailey and hurried to the door, snatching up his rifle on the way. 'Eliza, you stay here. I'll come back for you. And you,' – he turned to Bailey – 'you stay put and take care of the sheriff. Don't even think about leaving or so help me you're a dead man.'

CHAPTER
FOURTEEN

It sounded as if war had broken out. A crackle of rifle fire filled Cal's ears as he leapt off his horse and ran up the steep slope. He dived into cover a little below the lookout, hearing the louder bark of shots from above as the Rodway brothers returned the posse's fire. Getting himself snugged down, he stared through a gap between the rocks to take in the scene below.

The posse were making use of every scrap of natural cover they could find, mostly in the rocks on the opposite side of the gulch, where a dozen rifles were firing constantly, the shots echoing against the rock walls. Even at such a long range some of their shots were coming uncomfortably close, and Cal heard Bart yelp with surprise then swear long and loud when a slug zipped past him.

Marshal Gallagher wasn't stupid, he'd obviously listened to what the remnants of Macomber's posse had to say. Given the number of men he had, there was no need for him to take unnecessary risks, he had time to prepare the ground before he attacked. With the Rodway brothers forced to keep their heads down, only managing to snap off an occasional shot, several men were able to work in the shallow arroyo.

Cal had to admire the marshal's thinking. The posse were throwing up a screen of rocks to protect them, and the meagre cover where Cal had kept the solitary man in the red shirt pinned down was being turned into a stronghold. At that range they had a good chance of finding a gap in the outlaws' defences; their numbers and the ferocity of their attack must pay off in the end.

When he was ready, Gallagher could send riders to the ridge with the certainty that most of them would make it. Thanks to Bailey they would know about the gully; if they didn't locate the way around it they'd be prepared to abandon their horses and fight their way to the cabin on foot. The Hinds gang would be forced to retreat, with the thorn barrier as their last defence. There was only one way this battle could end.

The men who were digging and shifting stones in the arroyo were working fast, relying on the riflemen to give them cover, but occasionally one of them offered a clear target to the outlaws hidden above. Moke gave a triumphant shout as a member of the posse fell forward over the half finished wall, the back of his head a mess of bloody brains and splintered bone.

Another man, tall and heavily built, had been working alongside, stooping behind the growing wall of stone. As his neighbour dropped, he came suddenly upright to stare open-mouthed at the bloody corpse, his shovel falling to the ground. Cal drew a bead on the broad chest, then he hesitated. The big man wasn't even holding a gun, and he stood stock still in shock; it felt wrong to shoot him in cold blood.

Lowering his sights, Cal slapped a bullet into the rock wall beside the corpse. Instead of ducking into cover the man skittered backwards, as if in half a mind to retreat out of range. Before he could do so there was a crack from a rifle and a spray of red droplets erupted from his thigh. He staggered, half falling.

'Like knockin' tin cans off a log!' Moke crowed. 'Come on, Mason, you ain't tryin'.'

A fusillade of shots cracked and whined around Moke where he was hidden in the lookout and he ducked back, laughing. The injured man dragged himself towards the camp, then another member of the posse came to help, lifting the big man's arm over his shoulder and half carrying him out of range.

When there was a lull in the gunfire Cal lifted his head again to stare at the scene below. Moke was right: he had no stomach for this fight. They were ordinary decent men down there, men who sought justice for what the Hinds gang had done in Silverlode. And for the terror Moke and Bart had inflicted on those women at the ranch. The big man could be the husband of that young wife they'd terrorized. Cal's hands clenched as he thought how he'd feel if Moke so much as laid a hand on Eliza.

The rock wall along the arroyo was four feet high now, and several men were shooting from the cover it gave. In the lookout Bart was reloading, while Moke was cursing as he fired. The lawmen weren't taking any more chances and he had no hope of hitting anything.

Nearly half of the posse were grouped around the horses. It looked like Gallagher was ready to try the next part of his plan. Four more armed men ran across the open ground, coming from the far side of the gulch to dive into the arroyo. The sound of rifle fire became a continuous clamour again, as the rock face around the lookout came under a heavy barrage. Cal kept his head down and thought about Canada.

If he rode back to the cabin now he could pick up Eliza and make tracks before the Hinds gang knew he had gone. But there was Glenn Macomber to think of, and Seth Bailey. He might take young Bailey to safety, but the sheriff surely wasn't fit to sit a horse; even a short ride might kill him.

'Glad to see you aren't wasting lead,' Dobey Hinds commented, appearing suddenly at Cal's back. 'Bet that marshal thinks he's got us licked.' The usually benign expression was replaced by a ferocious grin. Hinds reached into his pocket for a cigar, striking a match against the rock to light it.

'Are you saying he hasn't?' Cal asked.

Hinds laughed. 'Marshal Gallagher's in for a shock. You reckon he'll be leading the charge himself? Even if he doesn't, with half his men buried under tons of rock I reckon he'll be leaving us real soon.'

'You took some stuff from a mine,' Cal said. 'Moke mentioned it. I guess you helped yourself to some dynamite.'

'And a few other bits and pieces. Come on, I'll show you.' Hinds led him down the slope a short way, to take a steep narrow track that ran around the flank of the hill and came out overlooking the gulch. From here they could see the whole length of the opposite ridge, and the path that wound to the top. Seeing them standing there, the men Gallagher had left at the mouth of the gulch aimed shots their way, but Cal and Hinds were well back inside the canyon, and at such long range nothing came near them.

Dobey Hinds pointed to a narrow split that cut the cliff below them from top to bottom. A piece of cord lay draped over the edge and disappeared into the shadows. 'I planted the explosive weeks ago, all I had to do was bring up the detonator and fuse. You and the boys were keeping the posse so busy I don't reckon they even saw me.' He turned, indicating another narrower crevasse a few yards away. 'There's another charge over there. I'm no expert, but I'd say this whole chunk of mountain will come down.'

'It looks that way.' Cal stared at the men moving like ants below. There was a constant rattle of gunfire from the arroyo, and the men at the horse line were mounted now. 'It'll block the canyon.'

'So nobody will be able to get to the ridge,' Hinds nodded, 'not unless they want to climb up the cliff, and if they try it we'll have all the time we need to pick them off.'

'Congratulations,' Cal said. 'I'd say you've out thought the marshal.'

'Yeah,' Hinds drawled. 'Which means you're going to have to come clean about how you got that kid to the cabin.' He turned away from Cal to shout across to Bart and Moke. 'They're mounting up, boys. Be sure and give them a warm welcome.'

'I told you,' Cal said, 'There's another way off the ridge.' He stared at the riders. If Hinds had his way all those men and horses would be dead in a few minutes. 'How long will it take the fuses to burn?'

'Less than a minute. Don't worry, I've got it figured

out. We'll have time to get clear. I light this fuse as the horses pass the arroyo, then go straight to the other one. The riders'll be flat out by then, seeing they won't want to give Moke and Bart an easy target. It's just as well bringing half the mountain down isn't going to leave us trapped.'

Hinds looked Cal straight in the eyes. 'I've ridden over all that high ground, and there's no other way off the ridge. You were lying, Mason. Not that I blame you, when a man's got a trump card he doesn't want to be in any hurry to show his hand, but we're going to need that trail out of the valley. You ready to tell me where it is?'

'It's well hidden,' Cal replied. He'd known this was coming. 'I could show you.' The riders were starting their move. If he was going to prevent a dozen more murders then he had to do something, and fast. But he didn't want the posse to reach the valley, any more than Hinds did. If those men reached the top of the ridge he'd very soon be dead.

From the arroyo the firing rose to a new crescendo. Over the din, Moke suddenly let out a great howl. Bart had fallen backwards, somersaulting away from the lookout to slide head first down the steep rocky slope.

Taking advantage of the distraction, Cal snatched the cigar from Hinds and leapt to slap it down hard against the end of the fuse, hearing the sizzle as it caught light. Hinds shouted in fury, landing a solid punch on Cal's cheekbone while his other hand tried a grab at the cigar. Dodging aside, Cal ran, heading for the other fuse with Hinds right behind him. He was almost there when hands grasped his arm and swung him off course.

'Let me go,' Cal said breathlessly, struggling to keep his

feet as Hinds slammed a fist into his ribs, 'they both have to blow or the cliff might not come down. You want that posse to get in here?'

'Damn you!' Hinds snarled, but he stepped back and Cal stabbed down with the crumpled butt of the cigar. Again he heard the fuse start to crackle as it burnt. He turned away, gesturing to Hinds.

'We'd better get out of here.' They ran together, heading back to the lookout.

Bart lay staring at the sky through one sightless eye. A splinter of rock protruded from the other socket, bloody fluid oozing around it and trickling over his face. Moke was still firing furiously at the advancing riders, screaming obscenities as tears ran down his cheeks. He emptied the gun and snatched up Bart's fallen weapon. Cursing when he found it too was out of ammunition, he flung the gun away, sending it spinning out over the canyon to career down onto the rocks, where the butt smashed off the barrel before it clattered to a stop on the dusty ground below.

The horsemen passed the arroyo, galloping hard, some of them whooping and cheering. Then the whole cliff exploded outwards, with a great blast of hot air, and a thunderous noise that totally eclipsed the sound of gunfire. The tumbling avalanche of rock, and the advancing riders, vanished in an enormous cloud of dust.

Awed by the sheer scale of the noise and blinded by the billowing haze, the three men in the lookout were stunned to silence. The mountain trembled beneath their feet. A few moments later a hail of small rocks showered down on them and they ducked beneath the overhang, their arms held defensively over their faces.

Cal thought he'd been deafened by the explosion for, as the dust began to thin, there was a strange quietness. Then, as if at a great distance, he heard the scream of a horse. Almost at once the faint crack of a shot echoed into the hills, and all was silent again.

'Hell!' Moke pushed past Cal. 'Let's take a look-see.' Hinds nodded, retracing his steps, and Cal fell in behind them.

The rough track ended before they reached the place where Cal had lit the fuses, the ground falling away to a great jumble of fallen rock. As the dust settled they could see that the avalanche had half filled the gulch with huge boulders. Nobody would ever ride through there again. Even a man on foot would have to climb a steep slope of loose stone to reach the ridge.

Down at the posse's camp there was chaos. Loose horses were running free across the prairie, bolting in terror from the falling torrent of rock. Most of the men who had managed to stay with their mounts were trying to gather in the others. Only one had ridden back to the landslide. He soothed his restive horse as he spoke to the men scattered around the arroyo. Cal recognized him as the man who had led the charge across the prairie when the posse arrived.

'That must be Gallagher,' Hinds said, voicing Cal's thought. 'You want to tell me why you're so keen on saving his life?' Something hard and cold was thrust into the middle of Cal's back. Hinds took the Henry from Cal's hand, and Moke came to jerk the Smith & Wesson from its holster.

'I told you he's a lawman,' Moke growled. 'You shoulda listened.'

'Don't be a fool,' Cal said, 'you got what you wanted, that trail's blocked.'

'I wanted them dead,' Hinds said. 'Especially Gallagher. He's too damn clever. Come on, if they put men on that slope we'll be easy pickings. Let's get back to the lookout.'

Cal turned around to face him and Hinds stepped back, the six-gun he held pointing unwaveringly at Cal's chest. The outlaw jerked his head. 'Move.'

Back behind the sheltering wall of the lookout they watched as the posse set about restoring order. Some of the horses had been recaptured, and an injured man was being carried in from the rock-strewn ground at the foot of the landslide. 'He's a lucky man,' Hinds remarked, as Gallagher led his horse away.

'That weren't luck,' Moke growled. 'You said it yourself, Dobey, Mason saved his hide.'

'Well?' Hinds demanded, his revolver still levelled at Cal. 'You'd better have a good reason for what you just did.'

'Murdering a dozen men just to keep them off your heels stuck in my craw,' Cal said. 'Didn't seem right.'

'You sayin' you got religion?' Moke shook his head, his silver eyes alight with fury. 'I don't buy it. Still say I was right the first time, you gotta be a lawman.'

'Lawman or not, he's the one who can get us out of here,' Hinds said, 'the same way he fetched Bailey.'

Cal shrugged. 'Sure, there's a way out of the valley. But Gallagher doesn't know that. Could be we can just wait them out.'

'Like Hell we will,' Moke said. 'We're leavin', an' real soon. We ain't gettin' trapped in here. '

'We're not trapped,' Cal said. 'But we're safe, for a time at least.'

'Me and Moke maybe,' Hinds said, a cold smile on his face, 'but I wouldn't take any bets on you.'

CHAPTER FIFTEEN

'I didn't never trust him,' Moke growled. He held Cal's six-gun in his hand, and as he spoke he whipped the barrel hard across Cal's face. Hampered by Hinds, who had just finished binding his wrists behind his back, Cal's attempt to duck aside didn't take him out of range, and the gunsight slashed his cheek to the bone. A second blow followed the first, this time hitting him on the forehead, just below the scar left by Hambo's bullet. The world spun.

Moke was grinning as he hit out yet again, striking down at the top of Cal's skull. Falling, seeing Moke still coming after him, Cal tried to roll out of the way, but he slammed into Bart's body. Breath whistled painfully from Cal's lungs as Moke's boot stamped down on his belly. In turn Cal lashed out with his feet, but Moke stepped aside, a vicious kick narrowly missing Cal's face.

'Careful,' Hinds cautioned, 'we need him alive.'

'Hell, if he can find Shorty's trail then so can we,' Moke sneered, dancing lightly away from Cal's feeble attempt to retaliate and lashing out with his boot again.

Cal jerked away and, while Moke was off balance, he managed to get a knee to the ground and heave himself half upright, only to get another pistol whipping as Moke crowded in on him again, an evil smile on his lips. Summoning all his remaining strength Cal surged upright, slamming the top of his head into Moke's nose.

Moke reeled back, swearing as blood dripped down his face. Cal staggered away from him, dodging past Hinds and jumping awkwardly over Bart's corpse, to hurtle recklessly down the hill towards the horses. He didn't get far. Moke came after him and brought the six-gun down hard at the base of his neck.

There was a second of darkness, a sensation of spiralling through a long black tunnel, then the pain in Cal's abused body returned and he was lying face down on the rocky ground, trying desperately to get back on his feet.

'What's the matter, Mason, ain't you happy in my company? You need some help there?' Moke gripped the rope holding Cal's wrists and pulled upwards, forcing his arms out behind his back, heaving them up until he gasped with agony. Sounds became echoes and the day darkened as unconsciousness beckoned.

Letting Cal go, Moke rolled him onto his back, cocked the six-gun and drilled it into his throat. 'I'm havin' a good time, but I'd as soon see you dead.'

Cal tried to focus on the face looming over his. Moke's crazy silver eyes were filled with an unholy light.

'You got any last words, Mason? Maybe you wanna leave a message for that little wife of yours. I sure am lookin' forward to gettin' to know her. Nothin' to say, huh?'

'Wait.' Hinds had come running down to them. 'I told you, Moke, we still need him. For now.'

His bruised face stiffening, Cal forced words past the gun barrel boring into his windpipe. 'Wise move,' he croaked. His life hung on getting through to Hinds. 'It took me four days to find that trail. Could be Gallagher won't give you that long.'

'He's right,' Hinds said shortly, as Moke started to argue. 'Fetch the horses. We're clearing out.'

'What about Bart?' Moke turned to look at his brother's body. 'I ain't leavin' him for no damn posse to find.'

'No place to dig, but there's plenty of rock. We'll use that hollow.' Hinds pulled out a knife and slit the ropes from Cal's wrists. 'You heard. Make yourself useful. Step out of line and I'll hand you back to Moke.'

Tied belly down over the black's saddle, Cal spent the short ride from the lookout drifting in and out of consciousness. At the cabin Moke dragged him to the ground, giving him a kick as he landed. Lifting him by the front of his shirt, Moke leant down to speak close in Cal's ear.

'Dobey's soft,' Moke said, 'but I ain't. But you don't have to worry, I changed my mind about killin' you yet awhile. I decided I ain't in any hurry, Mason. Remember I was tellin' you about that Apache? I was real sore when you didn't want no help entertainin' the sheriff. But I figure you an' me can have some fun, you can ride along with us for a day or two, that posse ain't gonna know we're gone. An' you can watch me havin' myself a good time with your wife. You'll maybe learn somethin'. I guess Eliza's gonna be real eager to please me, huh?'

Cal didn't answer. His head was pounding, but he had to think. Glenn Macomber was out of action and Bailey wasn't likely to put up any resistance. That left Eliza; he had to find a way to get her out of Moke's reach. At least with Bart gone there was only Dobey and Moke to reckon with. Cal twisted, trying to free his hands, praying that Eliza had seen them coming and had the sense to run.

Moke laughed as he disappeared into the cabin on Hinds' heels. Once they'd gone Cal struggled to his feet. Tied at the ankles, the best he could manage was a slow shuffle as he set course for the feed shed. He gritted his teeth as dizziness stopped him, determined not to waste precious time by falling. He'd only just made it to the open door when he heard footsteps behind him, and he twisted out of the way as Moke pushed past. There was nobody inside, and the bedroll where Glenn Macomber had lain had gone.

'Where'd they go?' Moke demanded, grabbing Cal by the throat.

'They aren't in the cabin?' Cal's bruised lips sketched a smile, so great was his relief. Somehow Eliza had got away. Briefly he wondered if the posse's attack had been a feint, and some of them had ridden in through the canyon, but that didn't make sense. They'd still be here; they'd have lain in ambush, waiting for the outlaws to ride into their trap.

'You know damn well they ain't in the cabin,' Moke shouted, his fingers squeezing Cal's neck. 'I'm givin' you just this one chance, an' you'd better tell me, or you die right here. Where is she?'

Words formed in Cal's head but he couldn't get them out.

'Talk!' Moke flung him away and Cal reeled, sagging against the door post.

Cal drew in a painful breath. 'Gone, you crazy sonovabitch,' he said. 'Eliza's gone. She knew about Shorty's

137

trail, she must have decided to get out. I guess Bailey helped her.'

'Moke!' Hinds appeared from the cabin, carrying a sack of provisions. 'Come on, fetch the other horses out of the barn. We're leaving.'

'No.' Moke was staring into Cal's face, his mouth twisting angrily. 'He's holdin' out on me. None of the horses has gone. Them two lawmen have to be around some-place, which means the girl's here too.'

'Never mind the girl, we don't have time. Hell, with the money we got in Silverlode you can buy yourself all the women you want. Put Mason back on that horse, so he can show us Shorty's trail. We'll ditch him once we're in the clear, maybe leave him for the posse. They can string him up if they've a mind to. It'll keep them off our trail a while longer.'

'I want the girl,' Moke said stubbornly. 'It's gonna be hours before that posse even tries climbin' up to the ridge. They'll figure we're waitin' for 'em; they won't risk gettin' picked off on them rocks. You go ahead an' ride if you want, I'm stayin' right here. I'm gonna make Mason talk.'

Hinds tied the bag to his saddle and looked up at the sky. 'Maybe Gallagher won't move till the morning.' Coming over to them he grabbed Cal's face, fingers goug-ing painfully into the cuts left by Moke's pistol whipping. He stared into Cal's eyes. 'You heard him. No woman's worth another beating. You don't want him to play rough, then you'd better tell us where they've gone.'

Cal summoned up a laugh. 'You want the honest truth? I don't know. But wherever they've gone, I sure hope they've got the sense to stay there, because come tomor-row this whole valley is going to be swarming with lawmen.

That posse won't sit there waiting out the night. I've been thinking about it. Gallagher's real smart. He'll figure we've got another way out of the valley, and you can bet he'll be looking for it. Maybe if they ask around someone out there will remember old Shorty. They'll know he ran a herd of cattle up here. You ready to let Moke tell you what to do, Dobey? I thought you were the one with the brains. Put me back on my horse and let's get out of here while we can.'

'That's enough!' Moke's voice lifted to a shriek. 'Dobey, you ain't gonna let him fool you?'

Hinds shrugged. 'Tell you what I'll do, Moke. It'll be dark in a couple of hours. I'll go back up to the lookout, see what's going on down there. If he's right and that marshal looks like he's making a move, then I'll come right back and we ride out. If not, then you can play with Mason a while. But don't forget he's got to be fit to show us that trail. If I come back and he's nothing but crow bait then I'll have your hide, boy.'

He turned back to stare Cal in the face again. 'Was I you, I'd think again. It could be a long night.'

Cal was hurting. The beating Moke had given him up at the lookout had been only the start. He couldn't recall everything that had happened since, like how he came to be strung up to a beam in the barn, his arms straining as they took his weight. Feeling was gone from his hands as the rope bit deeper into his wrists. His shirt had been pulled open at the front, and blood trickled slowly from open wounds on his shoulders and chest where strips of skin had been sliced away. Moke had fetched a bag of salt from the cabin; he seemed to find it amusing to rub the coarse white crystals into Cal's raw flesh.

Pain had made Cal's very existence a blur, and he'd hardly noticed that the daylight was beginning to fade, until he realized that only the shape of the doorway showed clear, the barn itself filling with shadows.

'Fact is,' Moke said, not much more than a shadow himself as he stood back, considering his next move, 'there's parts of a man that ain't so tough as others. You must've noticed that, huh?' He threw his knife, the blade stained red with Cal's blood, so it stuck quivering in the floor, then removed the rope that had tethered Cal's ankles. 'That ole Apache, he taught me a whole lot. But you don't have to worry, 'cos they reckoned to keep a man alive an' kickin' for weeks. Just one night ain't nothin'.'

Making an effort, Cal focused on the man before him. Moke was no longer wearing his gunbelt, it was hanging on a nail by the door, and at that moment his knife was on the floor by his feet. For some reason that was important, and Cal tried to remember why. Sometime he must have had a plan, an idea that needed Moke to be unarmed.

As Moke half straightened it came to him. Ignoring shoulders already strained to screaming point, Cal swung his legs around Moke, gripping his neck between his thighs. Cal had spent a lifetime in the saddle and his legs were all muscle. With his back protesting and his shoulders a red hot agony, he held on, squeezing with all his strength. His life depended on not letting go.

Moke's hands came up, digging into Cal's thighs. He stretched back, trying to reach the gashes on Cal's chest. Cal grimaced, sucking in a great gasp of air as Moke's fingernails raked into the raw wounds, but he clung on, tightening his grip.

Finding himself held as if in a vice, Moke screamed, his words echoing to the high roof. 'Dobey! Help me! Get in here! Dobey!'

Hinds might already be on his way back; he wouldn't stay in the lookout once night had fallen. Moke went on yelling. Cal's shoulders were being torn apart and there was a dimness before his eyes that had nothing to do with the setting of the sun. He willed himself to hang on, to ignore the pain; he mustn't pass out.

Legs thrashing, Moke was still making a noise, though the strangled sounds issuing from his throat were no longer recognizable as words. In desperation, maybe realizing the strain Cal was under just holding his own weight, Moke lifted his feet off the floor, his hands bearing down on Cal's thighs, his legs swinging.

An involuntary scream was forced from Cal's lips as he felt sinew and muscle tear under the added burden of Moke's weight. Jagged lightning strikes flashed across his vision; he couldn't hold on much longer. There was a roaring in his ears, then a steady rhythmic thud, growing ever louder.

A man came running into the barn. Cal was close to losing consciousness; he'd failed. His muscles loosened their hold. Moke half fell then reeled out of his reach, breath rasping in his throat, hands fluttering around the bruised flesh. He sagged to the ground for a moment, then rose, turning back towards Cal. His face contorted with pain and fury, Moke bent to retrieve his knife from the floor.

Cal's eyes blinked open. In a brief moment of clarity he saw that it wasn't Dobey Hinds who stood in the doorway. This was a larger man, younger. It was Seth Bailey. 'His gun,' Cal croaked urgently. 'There, on the nail.'

Bailey didn't need telling twice. He stepped over to where the holster hung on the wall, drew the pistol and levelled it. Moke, seeing death staring him in the face, flung himself to one side. He was far too late. The report of the Colt echoed around the barn. The bullet struck Moke full in the chest and he spun around, arms outflung, mouth open, staggering a few steps back towards Cal. The disquieting silver eyes held a puzzled expression, then they clouded over and he fell to sprawl lifelessly at Cal's feet.

Bailey stared down at the dead man for a brief moment, then picked up the fallen knife. He had slashed halfway through the rope that suspended Cal from the roof when another shot blasted the silence. Dimly aware of what had happened, Cal saw Bailey drop away from him, the knife slicing uselessly at the air. Dobey Hinds stood in the doorway, a smoking rifle in his hands.

'So, Moke was right, they were still here.' Hinds picked up the knife and finished cutting Cal down. Cal moaned as he fell. Hitting the ground was agony and lying on it wasn't much of an improvement. There wasn't a part of his body that didn't hurt.

'I ought to kill you right now.' Hinds said bitterly.

Reluctantly Cal opened his eyes. He was lying alongside Seth Bailey. A bloody wound high on the youngster's chest was leaking blood into the dust; the bullet must have passed straight through his body. Bailey's eyelids were flickering, the fingers of one hand flexing. Reviving a little, Cal found he was glad the kid was still alive. Keeping him that way looked to be a problem.

CHAPTER SIXTEEN

Cal rose to his knees, fixing his gaze on Hinds, willing him not to notice Seth Bailey, bleeding but still conscious, though barely. The kid had saved his life: the least he could do was try to repay that debt. The outlaw had stepped back, but at any moment he might realize Bailey was alive.

It took a gargantuan effort to get to his feet, and Cal swayed, taking a few uncertain steps towards the doorway with Hinds retreating warily in front of him, the rifle in his hands rock steady, his finger on the trigger.

'You won't kill me. That trail's not easy to find,' Cal said, grimacing as he pulled his shirt over the raw bloody patches on his chest, fumbling to fasten a couple of buttons with hands coming painfully back to life as the blood began pumping through them again. 'I'll show it to you, right now if you want, though I might need a hand to get into the saddle.'

Hinds shook his head. 'Not now, the light's almost gone. That posse don't look like moving tonight, though they might try an attack at first light. We'll go as soon as there's enough moon to see by.'

'Sure.' Cal made it to a stall and clung to the wooden

planks, waiting for the barn to stop spinning around him. 'Whatever you say.'

'Yeah, that's right. What I say. Maybe Moke was right about you, maybe not, but I'm taking no more chances.' He stalked to the doorway and stood framed in the last of the light. 'Hey, girl,' he shouted. 'I know you're out there. You ever want to see this husband of yours alive again, then you'd better show yourself, right now.' His eyes still on Cal, he moved on out of the barn.

'No!' Cal lurched towards him. 'There's no need for that. Hell, I told you, I'll show you the trail, right now if you want . . .' He was through the doorway, clutching at the hitching rail, Hinds' horse snorting and pulling back to the end of its rein, upset by the scent of blood. 'Eliza! Everything's gonna be fine. Don't you pay him no mind, stay right where you are!'

'Shut up, Mason.' Hinds backed off a couple more paces and shouted again, turning to scan the cabin and the rock face towering above it. 'I'm warning you, girl! You come on out.'

A slight figure appeared round the side of the cabin, hesitant at first. 'Cal!' Seeing him Eliza came running, dodging past Hinds as if she intended to fling herself into his arms, jolting to a standstill and staring in horror at the damage Moke's pistol whipping had done.

'Eliza.' His heart lurched, loving her, despairing of her. 'Won't you ever listen to me?'

She came to him then, tears spilling down her cheeks, her hands lifting towards his battered face, stopping as if afraid to touch him, gently fingering the blood beginning to seep through his shirt. 'Oh, Cal!'

He stared over the girl's head at Hinds, his expression

bleak. 'You hurt her and I swear I'll kill you,' he said, 'even if I have to climb up out of my grave to do it.'

'That's what it'll take if either one of you tries anything,' Hinds said. 'Where were you hiding, girl? Where's Macomber?'

'In the cave.' Eliza had taken one of Cal's hands. 'He's dead.' Her fingers squeezed gently, once, twice, as if to convey some message to him. 'Seth insisted on taking him in there, but the move killed him. That bullet must have damaged his lung. He choked on his own blood.'

'So, he's dead,' Cal said. 'Guess Bailey wasn't much of a medicine man after all.'

'Show me,' Hinds demanded, gesturing at Eliza with the rifle.

'We'll need a light,' Eliza said, taking a reluctant step towards the entrance. 'I couldn't see a thing in there this last while.'

'Go fetch one,' Hinds ordered. 'And no tricks. Your husband's going to be right out here with me.'

'You won't mind if I come and pay my respects?' Cal asked. 'The man's been on my heels for six months, sure would like to know he won't be troubling me no more.'

Hinds nodded, and when Eliza returned he ordered her to lead the way. Obediently she took him to the crack in the rocks, ducking down, pushing the lighted lamp inside and crawling after it.

'You next,' Hinds said, gesturing at Cal. He propped the rifle against the rock and drew his six-gun. 'And don't think of trying anything.'

A shrouded shape lay in the corner of the cave. In the flickering light from the lamp it almost looked as if it moved.

'Lift that blanket.' Hinds ordered.

Eliza shook her head and backed as far away as she could, the light swinging wildly. 'No. I. . . .'

'I'll do it,' Cal said, moving between Macomber and the light. The sheriff lay on his belly. Beneath his face was a cloth stained dark with blood. Cal laid a finger on the man's neck. 'Not cold yet,' he said, straightening. The pulse had been strong and steady, and he felt a surge of hope. 'He's dead right enough. Got away easy in the end, but at least he won't be bothering me no more.'

Flinging the blanket over Macomber's head again, Cal waited for Hinds to crawl back into the open. As soon as the outlaw had gone he leant close over Macomber's body, saying a few quick words in a low voice before he moved to follow.

'How come Bailey took you both in there?' Cal asked, struggling stiffly back to his feet, waving Eliza away as she bent to help him.

'Once he'd done all he could for the sheriff Seth came after you,' Eliza said. 'I think he had some idea about trying to get a message to the posse, though I told him it was crazy. Pretty soon he came running back. He wouldn't tell me what he'd seen, but he said we had to hide.'

Her eyes looked huge in the darkness. 'You'd told me there was a cave along the cliff here, and it didn't take us long to find it. We heard the horses and knew you'd come back. When somebody rode away again I wanted to look, to see who it was, but Seth wouldn't let me. Then Macomber died, and we sat here as it grew dark, listening.' She shivered. 'When . . . when we heard . . . Seth told me to stay here while he went to see what was happening.'

Cal took her in his arms. 'Sure am sorry,' he said softly.

'Young Bailey got himself killed saving my neck.'

At last she began to cry. 'I thought you were dead! And I stopped caring if I died too, because I don't think I could live without you.'

'Hush,' Cal said, stroking her hair. 'I'm here.' Across her head his eyes met Hinds' gaze in the growing darkness.

'Just don't forget who's holding all the cards,' Hinds said. 'Inside, both of you. Fix us a meal, girl, and make a pot of coffee. There's time before the moon rises, and we've got a long ride ahead.'

They rode out a couple of hours later. Cal had his hands tied to the saddlebow, with his horse's rein hitched to Hinds' saddle, while Eliza came behind leading a horse loaded with supplies. Back in the makeshift corral where they'd left the remaining horses, Moke's pinto, white patches shining in the moonlight, careered wildly along by the fence, neighing loudly.

'That damn paint's nearly as crazy as Moke was,' Hinds commented, as his own mount neighed in reply. He dragged on Cal's rein to bring his horse closer alongside. 'Just so the pair of you know the score,' he said, turning his head to be sure Eliza could hear, and patting the carbine in the holster by his knee, 'if you try anything, girl, it's Mason that gets the bullet. You understand?'

'Yes.' Eliza's voice was meek. 'I understand. All I want is for us to get out of here safely. Cal's the only thing that matters to me.'

Cal sat slackly in the saddle, slumped over as if he was in danger of falling off. He was still hurting but he felt a whole lot better with food and three cups of strong coffee inside him. After they'd eaten Eliza had insisted on treating Cal's hurts. When Hinds argued she'd pointed out that Cal was no use to him dead, and Hinds had reluctantly agreed.

Eliza had been gone a long time when she went to fetch Seth's bundle of medical supplies from the cave, and while she was bathing the wounds on Cal's chest she'd taken one of his hands briefly and given it two squeezes, just as she had when she lied to Hinds about Macomber's death. He'd looked up at her, frowning a warning; Hinds was no fool, they had to be careful. Eliza bit her lip and dropped her gaze.

Later, as she obeyed Hinds' order to pack some food, Eliza had looked across at Cal, a smile in her eyes. Cal's heart beat a little faster. What Eliza had said to Hinds went double for him; he'd value no part of his life unless this woman was in it. For as long as he lived he wanted her at his side.

The faint trail unwound slowly under the horses' hoofs. They kept to a walk, working their way slowly up the valley. Hinds stared at the mountain looming every closer at their side, a great dark shadowed beast crouching above them in the moonlight. 'You sure there's a way through?' he asked at last.

Cal took his time answering. Hinds thought he was pretty much out on his feet, and he saw no reason to disillusion him. 'Sure,' he said at last, wearily, as if even talking was painful. 'But we've got a way to go. We have to find the old wagon wheel, that's the only marker Shorty left. Be a few miles yet.'

'A wheel?'

'Half buried in the dirt. Guess the rest of the wagon's

hidden up here someplace too, maybe it got buried by an avalanche. Weather gets rough later in the year, they used to have a whole lot of snow in winter.'

By the time they located the wheel and turned into what looked like just one more blind canyon, Hinds was getting rattled. The eastern sky was showing light, and the moon was sinking behind the hills. He suddenly drew his pistol, pointing it first at Cal and then at Eliza. 'Remember what I told you, Mason. If you're trying to make a fool out of me, if there's no way out of here. . . .'

'There's no need for threats,' Cal said wearily. 'I told you, this trail took some finding. Four days I rode up and down every one of these canyons. Damn near gave up before I got to the end of this one. Half an hour, Dobey, and you'll be looking across fifty miles of open country, I swear it.'

Hinds nodded, slipping the weapon back into its holster. 'Move on then. But let's—'

At that instant a meadowlark rose from beneath the hoofs of the pack horse. It threw up its head in alarm, jerking back and pulling the lead rein from Eliza's hand. Taking fright in its turn, Eliza's mount careered into Cal's black. For a split second they were side by side. Cal felt something hard and cold against the back of his fingers; at the cost of a few more scraps of skin rubbed off his wrists he grabbed the thing and hid it between his hands.

'Get that fool horse back here!' Hinds yelled, hauling Cal's rein to pull his horse closer. He drew his six-gun again. 'And make it fast!' Obediently Eliza turned, sending her mount loping after the pack animal. Taking advantage of Hinds' distraction as he watched Eliza, Cal risked a quick look at the object she'd given him, just visible in the light spilling into the eastern sky. It was a knife, horn handled, tucked in an ancient leather sheath. He recognized it, had seen it many times before: it belonged to Glenn Macomber.

Dawn had painted the prairie sky in a hundred shades of pink and gold. The three riders sat their horses at the top of the trail that followed a meandering route down to the plain.

'That's beautiful,' Eliza breathed.

Cal glanced at her, praying this wouldn't be the last sunrise she ever saw. He'd moved the knife to his sleeve, where it dug into the raw flesh above his wrist. There had been no chance to use it, no moment when Hinds' eyes were off him long enough to cut the ropes that held his hands together and bound him to the saddlebow.

'How far from here to where the posse's camped?' Hinds asked.

'I'm not sure,' Cal replied. 'Could be five miles, could be ten.' He would have to act soon; Hinds didn't need guidance to find his way from here. Down on the prairie a man could move faster, although the posse was between Hinds and everywhere he was likely to want to go. To stay in the clear he would have to ride south, back towards Kentville. One thing was sure: he wouldn't want to leave Cal and Eliza behind to tell Gallagher where he was headed.

'Look!' Eliza shouted suddenly, pointing into the distance. Far off, where the land dropped away to the north, a little colunm of what looked like smoke was lifting into the still morning air. 'Is that a fire?'

Hinds shifted his horse to stare that way, and Cal slid

the knife from its sheath. He'd had hours to think about how it should be done, but his fingers were stiff, refusing to grip.

'That's not smoke, it's dust. Riders.' Hinds spun round, pulling Cal's horse behind him. Cal lurched at the sudden move. The hilt was between his hands, the blade resting on the rope that held his wrists. 'They know we're here! You found a way to double-cross me—'

'No!' Cal said, keeping his hands still as the man rounded on him. 'Gallagher's no fool, he's just playing safe.'

'I'm through with listening to you.' Hinds' face was twisted in fury. 'Maybe Moke was right and you've been playing a crooked hand the whole time. I figure you had this planned all along.' The outlaw's hand dropped to the butt of his six-gun.

'Eliza,' Cal shouted, 'get out of here! Now!'

'No!' Hinds whipped round to look for the girl. Seeing her kick back at her mount's flanks he wasted time holstering the six-gun in favour of his carbine. It gave Cal the few seconds he needed.

As the outlaw heaved the firearm from beside his knee Cal finally sliced through the ropes. With his hands free he gripped the hilt in his right hand, flexing his fingers around the horn. There was no time to wonder if Eliza had obeyed him, though he thought he heard hoofbeats drumming on the baked earth.

Hinds already had the carbine to his shoulder, taking aim. Frantically Cal kneed his horse towards the outlaw.

CHAPTER SEVENTEEN

Cal lunged, stabbing the knife into Hinds' back, up under the ribs, seeking for the man's heart. Hinds gasped, his body arching, but he didn't drop his gun. Terrified that the man might still shoot Eliza, Cal put every ounce of his strength behind his second thrust, burying the blade to the hilt.

The blast of sound as the carbine fired was deafening in Cal's ears. Hinds jarred backwards from the recoil, the horse beneath him spinning, taking the man out of Cal's reach, the knife's haft sticking obscenely from his back.

With a sigh that turned to a last weary rattle of breath, Hinds slumped and tipped sideways. His horse snorted, shying away as the body slid from its back, dragging Cal's mount with it. Unable to see Eliza, Cal leapt from the saddle. He fell as he landed, hitting his head.

It took Cal a moment to struggle dizzily to his knees. He looked around, desperate to find Eliza, but there was a mist before his eyes. That shot . . . Then came the sound of hoofbeats, a horse moving fast, and a blur of movement as somebody dismounted. She was alive. Looking up, expecting to see her, he found himself staring instead at the burly figure of Glenn Macomber. Behind him stood Moke's pinto, steam rising from its sweating flanks. The sheriff stepped across to Hinds' body. With care, as if the movement hurt him, he bent to pick up the carbine that lay beside the dead man.

Ignoring Macomber, desperate to know what had happened to Eliza, Cal got to his feet. His whole body sagged with relief as he saw her riding towards him, the pack horse alongside.

'Looks like you saved Gallagher some trouble,' Macomber said. He had Hinds' carbine in his hands, the muzzle pointing at Cal. 'You're gonna need that horse.'

'Good to see you, too, Glenn,' Cal said. 'Guess you're feeling better.'

'I'm feeling like hell.' Macomber growled. 'Come on, whistle up that black of yours. We'll go join the posse.'

'No!' Eliza came running to them, abandoning the two horses. 'You can't take him back, not now. Cal saved your life, twice.'

Macomber's face flushed red. 'I know it.'

'Then let him go!'

'I'm sorry, ma'am, the law don't work that way. He murdered a man. You can't just wipe that away like it didn't happen. I'll see he gets a fair trial.'

Eliza's eyes sparkled dangerously, but when she spoke her words seemed irrelevant. 'What happened to Seth?'

'He'll be fine. Reckon if I ask, Gallagher will send somebody to fetch him. And before you say it, I know Cal saved his neck too. Would have bled to death if I hadn't tended him as soon as the three of you were out of the way.'

Eliza said nothing, and Macomber was almost pleading

as he went on. 'Look, I'll stand up in court and make sure the jury knows what Cal did. An' I'll swear that killing Mort was . . . Hell, I don't know what it was,' he finished, turning furiously on Cal. 'Why d'you do it?'

Cal sighed. 'Wish I knew,' he said.

Macomber gaped. 'Are you loco? You claim you were drunk or something?'

'He's lost his memory,' Eliza said.

'How come?'

'I met up with Hambo and Titch Wilkie,' Cal said. 'Pair of 'em came riding up to the cabin before the Hinds gang got back from Silverlode. They decided the hideout would be a better place without me in it, didn't wait to introduce themselves before they started throwing lead.'

'They're dead?' Macomber asked.

'Feeding the coyotes.' Cal nodded, touching the scar on his forehead. 'Trouble was, this crease sent me crazy. When I came to my senses there were a whole lot of things missing from my past. Including my reasons for shooting Mort Bailey.'

Macomber scowled, shifting his feet a little and wincing. 'Look, we can jaw about this once we're on our way, it's been a long night. Miss Prentice, I'd be obliged if you'd help round up those horses.'

'No,' Eliza said. 'Not unless we're heading back to the valley.'

'What for?' Macomber stared down towards the prairie. The little group of riders were still heading south. 'Guess they didn't hear that shot. Maybe a couple more will fetch 'em.' He pointed the carbine into the air.

'No! Please!' Eliza pulled at his arm. 'We have to get back and talk to Seth. He knows something. Maybe he evens knows why Cal killed that man.'

'Seth? What can he know? The kid didn't reach the ranch until Mort had been dead a week.'

'Yesterday, when we were getting that bullet out of your back, he started to tell me about something that happened the day Cal pulled him from under his dead horse, up on the ridge. Seth's feeling guilty about it, and I'm certain it has to do with his uncle. Please, Sheriff. We have to go back.'

Macomber looked doubtful.

'Mac, you and me have been friends a long time,' Cal said. 'Let's all go to the cabin so we can talk to Seth – that's all we're asking. If it turns out we're wrong then I'll come back to Bannack County, quiet as a lamb.'

'We'll be so grateful—' Eliza began, breaking off suddenly. 'Sheriff, you were crazy to come riding after us. Look at you!' She pointed at the back of his shirt, which was dark with blood. 'You'd best let me see if I can stop the bleeding, because otherwise you'll be going nowhere.'

'And I ain't got the strength to make a decent job of burying you,' Cal said, summoning up a grin. 'Best do as the lady says. Be real inconvenient you dying just now.'

'You did right bringing him back.' Seth Bailey let Eliza help him to his feet. 'If he'd gone on bleeding like that I doubt if the sheriff would ever have made it back to Bannack County. He needs a few days' rest.'

'Lot of damn fuss over nothing,' Macomber growled, but he didn't try to move.

'How about you, Seth?' Cal asked, leaning his weight on the table. The way he felt, a few days rest sounded like a swell idea. 'That bullet hole troubling you any?'

'It's mending clean,' the youngster replied. 'I'd prescribe the same treatment.' He lowered himself carefully into the cabin's only chair. 'And for you, Mason.' Bailey jerked his head towards the bedroll in the corner.

'Well?' Glenn Macomber said. 'You planning to make a run for it?'

'No,' Cal replied, 'I'll be here when you're fit to travel. Guess I'll go with you and face trial, if that's what you want.' He licked his lips, his mouth suddenly dry.

'What do you say, Seth?' Macomber prompted. 'Mason here thinks you know why Mort Bailey died.'

Before the younger man could answer, the door opened and Eliza walked in. She was pale, struggling under the weight of the sack of provisions she'd taken from the pack horse; even her bright hair seemed dulled by exhaustion. Cal pushed upright to help her but she shouldered him aside, putting her burden on the table. 'I'll fix a meal in a minute . . .' She broke off, looking from one to the other, sensing the tension between them. 'What's wrong?'

Seth Bailey gave a sudden bitter laugh. 'It was all I ever wanted, to be a doctor. When my pa died I pinned all my hopes on Uncle Mort. I wanted a loan, told him I'd pay him back soon as I could. He wrote saying I could have a job at the ranch instead.' Bailey scowled. 'I hoped I could change his mind, but he was dead and buried by the time I got to the Bar Zee. I didn't know what to do. It was Mrs Bailey who persuaded me to join the posse.'

'Hope?' Macomber looked puzzled. 'She sent you after Cal? That's real strange, the reward was her idea too. She promised to pay if anybody claimed it.'

Bailey nodded. 'She wanted Mason dead. The way she

156

told it, he was too popular, and maybe the men chasing after him wouldn't have the heart to see it through, including you, Sheriff. Whatever happened, she didn't want him brought back for trial. She offered me a thousand dollars.'

'I knew Hope didn't feel too kindly,' Cal murmured, 'like it was my fault she turned her back on me and married Mort.'

Macomber's brow furrowed. 'You made her a widow, Cal.'

'I know it. But maybe it wasn't only Mort's death she wanted me to pay for. Go on, kid.'

'You know what happened. I came back with a broken leg, and you were still alive.' The youngster bit his lip and looked at Macomber. 'He sent you a message.'

Cal stared at him. Suddenly he could see it all in his head. The sun going down as he lowered Bailey off his back; the kid's pale defiant face. 'Yes! I remember! I wanted Glenn to talk to young Joe, Mort's boy. He was there that day!'

'But you never gave me any message,' Macomber said sombrely, looking up at the youngster, 'and you never told me about Cal saving your fool life that day.'

'I needed that money,' Bailey said wretchedly. 'I stayed at the ranch while my leg was mending, and Mrs Bailey never quit reminding me about that thousand dollars, how it was the only way I'd ever get to finish my medical training. Somehow she made sure the second posse didn't leave until I was fit enough to come along.'

'Is that true, Mac?' Cal asked.

Macomber nodded slowly. 'There was business to see to. She said she couldn't face it alone . . .' His face was hard as he looked at Bailey again. 'So, you didn't give me the message. But did you talk to young Joe?'

'Yes. Though I never got the whole story, because Mrs Bailey came and interrupted us. And after that she made sure we were never alone again. But I know Mason killed my uncle in self-defence.'

'That's not the way I remember it,' Cal said suddenly. 'He didn't have a gun in his hand when I shot him.'

'No. That was where his plan went wrong. Fate, I guess. He'd set everything up. He asked you to visit him when he knew nobody else would be around. He'd been spreading rumours for weeks about how you were broke, and how you blamed him for the cattle you'd lost in that stampede, when he and his men were taking the stock to the rail-head. It was supposed to look like you went there to rob him, and he killed you in self-defence.'

Bailey gave another bitter laugh. 'Only you got lucky. His gun misfired, and the discharge burnt his hand.'

'He dropped it.' Cal stared unseeingly at the young man, remembering at last. 'That gave me the chance to draw on him. If I'd let him live he'd have found a way to finish me; he couldn't let me tell the truth. I saw the boy looking in at the open window, just as I squeezed the trigger. Jeez, that poor kid.'

'But if he saw you kill his father. . . .' Macomber said.

'He heard the whole thing. And he saw his father try to shoot me before I drew on him.' Cal bit his lip. 'Joe climbed in through the window. Said he'd had an idea that something bad was going to happen. His father sent him out with Hope, but he persuaded her to come back.'

'There was no gun anywhere near Mort's body,' Glenn Macomber objected.

'No, Hope came in and took it,' Cal said. 'And she cleaned up the powder burns on his hand. She was ready to swear I'd killed him in cold blood. What choice did I have? I couldn't kill her and Joe. I had to run.'

'But why was she so desperate to hide what really happened?' Eliza asked.

'For money,' Cal replied. 'I wasn't the only one Mort cheated. That 'stampede' almost broke a lot of us smaller ranchers. But there was no stampede. Funny thing was I didn't see it, not till Mort told me. He didn't take his usual crew on that drive, he hired in a whole lot of hands from somewhere up north. And I guess they got a pretty big pay off when he sold the cattle that were supposed to have died on the way. If that ever came out, Hope Bailey would lose every cent Mort left her.'

'I can't let that happen.' Seth Bailey was suddenly on his feet. In his hands was Moke's long-barrelled Colt. He backed up towards the stove. 'I need my share of that money. I need what she promised me.'

There was a moment of stunned silence. It was Eliza who found her voice first. 'No, Seth. You can't do this. You saved the sheriff's life, taking that bullet out of his back. You're not a killer.' She took a step towards him.

'Stay where you are,' he said wildly, both hands on the gun now as he pulled back the hammer. 'Don't come any closer.'

'Or what? You'll shoot me? That's the only way you'll get your hands on that filthy money.'

'Eliza!' the word was a prayer, torn from Cal's dry lips. He was on his toes, his eyes fixed on the weapon, waiting for the faintest twitch of Seth's finger, 'Bailey. Don't—'

The crash of the shot was thunderously loud in the tiny

159

cabin. Cal threw himself forward, gathering Eliza into his arms as she fell back. Seth Bailey flung the gun down and ripped open the door, his footsteps fading into silence as he ran from them, ran from the person he had so nearly become.

A faint wisp of dust drifted down from the roof where the bullet had embedded itself in the dry old wood. Eliza twisted in Cal's arms and pressed her lips to his mouth, pulling free after a long breathless moment to smile at him. 'I told you I could look after myself,' she said. 'And this time I didn't even need a frying pan.'